TERRIBLE, HORRIBLE EDIE

By E. C. Spykman

To be the youngest of four children, and a girl at that, made life almost unbearable at times for ten-year-old Edie Cares. Theodore was eighteen—a godlike creature to Edie except that he infuriated her frequently by his air of superiority. Jane was seventeen and almost as bad, and Hubert—just turned sixteen—was a fickle companion at best. Edie kept hoping she would be included in their many activities, but she was always disappointed. In rebellion against this unjust fate, Edie was in almost constant trouble.

The summer the Cares children spent at the shore, when their father and stepmother went to Europe, was a memorable one for Edie—chiefly for the wrong reasons. There was the hilarious trip to the shore, with Hubert driving, which included fire, fog, and a brush with the law; the time Edie was caught in a sudden storm while sailing alone against all the rules; and her awe-

sorrows, its hopes and disappointments —which children and grownups alike will read with delight.

TERRIBLE, HORRIBLE EDIE

E. C. SPYKMAN

Elizabeth

Terrible,
Horrible
Edie

HARCOURT, BRACE & WORLD, INC., NEW YORK

F.II.68

21481

LIBRARY OF CONGRESS CATALOG CARD NUMBER: 60-8412

PRINTED IN THE UNITED STATES OF AMERICA

*To Kath who has made it possible for
me to write my books*

Contents

1. THE TRIP   9

2. TERRIBLE, HORRIBLE EDIE   48

3. MILLARD'S COVE   84

4. THE WEATHER   119

5. THE ENEMY   148

6. THE JEWELS   178

7. LOU   209

CHAPTER ONE

The Trip

"Everything will go in but the bird," Hubert Cares said, standing in front of his stepmother with his hands on his hips.

"The bird has to go, Hubert."

The John Cares family, which usually lived in The Red House in Summerton, Massachusetts, was trying to move to the beach. Whenever Aunt Louise decided to go to Europe, and that was quite often, Father borrowed her house at Mount Harbor, so that all of them, Theodore who was now eighteen, Jane who was one year younger, Hubert who was just sixteen, and Edie who was ten, knew about beaches, boats, swimming, eelgrass, and things like hermit crabs and tides. Even Madam, their stepmother, and her two little children, The Fair Christine who was five and Lou who was three, had paddled and sat in salt water. This year it was a great event because Hubert had been asked by Father to drive Edie down to the beach in the Ford, taking also the leftovers that had not gone into the hampers—like a few loaves of bread, a box of kitchen matches discovered at the last minute, some egg beaters, the salad bowl that never fitted anywhere, and the ice-cream freezer. Also there was the livestock—Madam's troupial, a fierce black bird called

Laza, Edie's goat, Theodore's spider monkey, and Father's beagle, Sport. All the livestock was enclosed in something, but still, as Hubert pointed out, it had to breathe now and then. Space had to be kept, for instance, between Jocko de Monk and the tremendous box full of milk, butter, and eggs on which the family would have to live for the first few hours after they arrived. The goat would want to be able to look out through his bars and enjoy the ride. It was much too small a goat to take traveling in Hubert's opinion, worse than Lou, who at least did not have to have a bottle every few hours. But Edie could keep on asking "Why?" or "Why not?" until nobody could think of any better reasons than her own, so there the goat was, baaing its objections to everything that was put on top of it. And now the Ford was piled so high there was not room for the trupial and his cage. Hubert would just as leave have left him at home too. He was a wicked bird, as you could tell by looking into his eyes, and he tried to bite everyone but Madam.

"If he got out," he had said to Edie when he was bringing the cage out, "he could easily put our eyes out before I could stop the car."

"Could he?" Edie asked anxiously as he had meant her to. "Do you think he could?"

But Madam would not give in. "There won't be anybody here to take care of him," she said. She was in the front hall standing in front of the big gold mirror with a pin in her mouth ready to put on her veil because Father liked to drive fast with the top down. They were going in the big Packard and taking everybody from the kitchen in the back seat. The kitchen department was already ready, sitting up very stiffly in the car right now—Gander the parlormaid, who had been in the family since anyone could remember, Cook, who came and went, and a girl no one knew the name of yet because she had come only yesterday. Probably she was to help the others when they felt lazy. They were dressed for the North Pole, although it was a perfectly good day in June with just a few clouds on the horizon. Besides their own clothes, they each had on a kind of yachting cap and veil and long white coats that Madam had bought them so they would not be settled on by a speck of dust. In between them somehow were stuffed The Fair Christine and Lou, unable to move or hardly to be seen on account of so many high elbows.

"Why can't the cage go on the floor of *your* car?" Hubert asked reasonably.

Madam looked at him, laughing over the pin. "He might peck their ankles," she said.

It made Hubert laugh too, but just the same he had to go back to the Ford, unpack everything, and fit it all together again as fast as he could, tucking the small things in nooks and crannies, to make more room. It would not do any harm, he decided, for the goat to look through a couple of sieves, or for Laza to have a few dish towels on top of his cage. The matches he stuck in a nice little hole at the bottom, out of the way of Jocko's long fingers. He was just about finished when Edie came round the corner of the barn with her dog, Widgy.

"I was just trying to catch a pigeon," she said. "We could send a message back to Grandfather."

"No!" said Hubert.

"Why not?"

Hubert was not going to be caught this time. Besides, somebody had given her a doughnut and she was eating it right under his face.

"Go get me one!"

"There aren't any more. Cook was cleaning out the cupboard. Here." She shoved the last bit into his mouth.

"It's not enough," said Hubert grumpily.

But it was time to go, and they went back to the hall to say good-by to Madam. Theodore and Jane had gone long ago on the train, conducting the wicker hampers with the linen in them to the place where they had to change trains in Charlottesville and getting them started off again in the right direction, and then waiting around the station to meet an unknown person by the name of Miss Jeananne Black to get her started in the right direction too. Miss Black, whoever she was, was to spend the summer with them at Aunt Louise's, because this time Father and Madam, as soon as their family was settled at the beach, had decided to go to Europe too. Life at the moment was very congested, Hubert felt, and would be even worse this evening when they all arrived at Aunt Louise's in a kind of torrent. He supposed sadly that it would take quite a while at that time for anybody to produce anything to eat. Butter and eggs at the moment seemed a flimsy sort of diet.

"And I'm hungry already," he said, getting behind the wheel.

"Let's stop at the drugstore then," said Edie, "and put in some supplies."

Their supplies were a box of marshmallows, two licorice

whips, five sticks of one-cent gum, and some chocolate creams.

"Not very filling, I must say," said Hubert. "I should have gone in myself."

So he stopped again at the end of the village. Father, when Nurse had got too old to take care of them, had set her up in a store, and besides papers of pins and threads and needles, she sold sausages in homemade buns, real sausages that came from the Home Farm and were spiced and had almost no skins, and real vanilla ice cream, not the thin foamy kind, with fresh-crushed strawberries. And also Father had given Hubert quite a fortune to take on the trip for gas, tires, and what he called "other eventualities." This was certainly one of them. Hubert had worked so hard that he needed a few of the comforts of life.

"Besides," said Edie, "they always say you shouldn't do things on an empty stomach."

"Or a full one," said Hubert, rubbing his. "It could be," he added brightly, "that you're not meant to work at all."

It all delayed them a little. They had to talk to Nurse and tell her the news. They didn't get started again for almost twenty minutes, but Hubert felt better.

"I must say, though, you do feel sleepy on a hot day after you've had a little something to eat."

"If you start going to sleep," said Edie, "I'm going to pinch you."

She kept her hand ready, watching Hubert and the road carefully, but after some terribly wide yawns and giving himself a few slaps in the face he seemed all right.

"The smell in here," he said, rubbing his nose finally instead of his eyes, "would keep anybody awake."

They had had to put on the side curtains and fasten them, even on this June day, because they had been strictly told by their owners that birds and monkeys did not like drafts. No one would mind about Laza particularly, they agreed, no matter what happened to him, but if Jocko got sick, they would be sorry. He had a really good-looking face for a monkey and as good manners as—well, Lou anyway— so they bowled along the back country roads with Hubert making the Ford go a little extra fast in order, he said, to keep the smell going backwards.

"This is not a bad little car," said Hubert, leaning back casually as they came out of a town called Broughton and giving the accelerator a twitch with his finger.

"If I were you, I would look out for hens, just the same," said Edie.

"I am not going to hit a single hen," said Hubert.

Edie was as much against scaring horses. The ones they met did not like it at all. They stood on their hind legs, or, if not that, began backing into the ditches or whacking their carts to pieces. People shouted after them angrily as they were swallowed up in a cloud of the Ford's dust. Edie felt sorry for them and said so.

"They'll have to get used to it in this life," said Hubert hardheartedly.

What he loved for the moment was the Ford and the way it leaped ahead the minute he touched the lever. He felt very responsible too, of course, with all these animals in the car. And, naturally, Edie. He meant to take care of everything, but he saw no reason why they shouldn't have a little fun too. Women—who could know better, with four sisters—were always nervous and he had no intention of letting it get him down.

It was the heat that began gradually to get them both down. It was always the same way. It might be fairly cool in Summerton, and at the beach it was never very hot—you could feel the wonderful coolness coming a long way away—but in the middle country between, although there were lots of big trees and sometimes even shady alleys in the little towns, it was always as hot as an oven. Hubert decided to distract himself as they raced along by seeing if he could hit and scatter the little piles of dirt the road men had piled up at the side of the road. Everything in the car was jerked and joggled, but that was probably a good thing, as it would settle things down and make them ride better.

Edie tried to forget the heat by looking at the daisy fields. It was a kind of forbidden pleasure. Nobody on the family dairy farms could possibly approve of them; it meant the land had gone sour, and daisies were weeds. Just the same, she thought disloyally, they were wonderful to look at. The whole middle country must have gone sour because it was full of them. She tried to open her eyes more than naturally so that she could see better. She wanted to remember how fat the trees were in this part of the world and she did not want to miss the farmhouse that somebody had painted pink—on the family dairy farms they would never have done such a thing as that either. There were lots of good things on this road. There was a dog hospital where the dogs were sometimes out in their yards in bandages; there was a cottage roof done with thatch, and a barn where they had the best bred bull in America who looked as if he could kill you any time. Maybe the best of all, in the dustiest, hottest, longest part, when there didn't seem to be a hope of anything for miles and miles, there might be a gypsy camp. She squinted as hard as she could through the blurry windows. Yup, they were coming to it. Caravans were gathered in a field with their horses tethered to them, there were little fires going, with pots hung over their tops, and all the women had costumes on and colored handkerchiefs round their heads. Her body followed the sight as it sped by and she tried hard to sniff the fires. She thought she could, but they did not seem to smell as good as usual. The old car itself was too hot and Widgy on her lap was like forty hotwater bottles. Hubert gave her a look. "Are you going to explode in a minute?" he said. "You look it."

"So do you," said Edie quickly.

Hubert slowed up. "We're going to get some air in here if all the monkeys in Christendom catch cold," he said, struggling with his window curtain. "Take yours off too; go on, turn the knobs and pull it off. Phew! That's a relief."

While they were going so slowly, Edie thought the smell from the gypsy fires was lasting a long time, or maybe the middle country was burning its leaves. She remembered at once, however, with a tiny shock that you didn't burn leaves in summer, *or* fields; it must be rubbish.

"Hubert," she said, "do you smell smoke?"

"Sure," he said calmly, "there must be a factory round here."

That was just what it smelled like. Anyway as soon as they began to go fast again, it went away and she almost went to sleep herself. She was woken up just as they were getting into a little town called Grampham, which was a whole mass of factories, by Jocko de Monk putting his hand through the cage bars and pulling her braid.

"Hey, stop it," said Edie, pulling it away.

She did not look round. Having a bird and monkey in the car, which could be plainly seen now that the curtains were off, made people on the sidewalks stare, and she did not want to encourage them. You could never tell what they would do. Theodore had told them that once when he was taking Jock somewhere a man had tried to open the cage and let him out. It was cruelty to animals, he had said. When, in the middle of Grampham, Hubert had to wait for a car ahead and people began pointing, she put on a face of being blind and deaf and looked straight ahead. She didn't see why they couldn't mind their own businesses.

"Gosh," said Hubert, rubbing his nose round and round with the palm of his hand, "don't those factories stink."

Just after he had said it, a man on the sidewalk called to them.

"Don't pay any attention to him," said Hubert. "He's trying to get fresh with you."

The man was fresher even than usual because he followed them half running. Edie tried not to, but for one minute she turned her eyes and ears toward him to see what he was like. She saw him put his hands to his mouth like a megaphone, and she listened. "Ye're afire," he called.

"What!" said Edie, leaning forward and squinching her face up.

"Ye're car's afire," said the man, "and if yer don't do somethin' about it pretty quick, ye're'll be afire yerselves."

Edie scrambled round to her knees in a flash. A thin solid piece of smoke was coming up from the floor between the ice-cream freezer and the eggs, right into Jocko's face.

"We *are* on fire, Hubert. What'll we do?"

Hubert looked back himself with a quick glance. "Hallelujah!" he said. "Let us be perfectly calm," he added as he pulled to the curb. "I hope the beagle's all right." Father's beagle was the farthest down because beagles never object to anything. "Look, see that drugstore. Go in and ask for a big glass of water. We can pour it down the hole. I'm not going to unload unless I have to. No, leave Widgy here. NO!" roared Hubert as Edie started to say something. "He'll get lost. Get a move on. But don't make yourself conspicuous." The car had stopped and Edie started to run before her feet touched the ground, but she stopped them right away and with dignified long strides crossed the sidewalk. It was terrible to know what to do, she thought, as she went. Men had no sense. She ought to be getting the fire department or all the animals would be fried to a cinder. What was the use of a glass of water? That would hardly put out a match! But how did you get the fire department in a town like Grampham?

Edie could not remember that she had ever had any prayers answered even when she had prayed them in the direst circumstances, but just after she said "God, please send the fire department," and had her foot on the drugstore step, she saw the red box on the corner. It took her one second to reach it and pull down the handle inside as she had often read in Charlottesville was the thing to do. Then she went into the store and asked for the water. When the glass was full, she picked it up carefully and made for the door with her dignified stride.

"Hey," said the druggist, "where you goin'?"

Edie didn't answer, but if she had, he couldn't have heard, because suddenly there was a long-drawn-out wail that sounded like a foghorn. "Say, ain't that the fire whistle?" said the druggist. Edie heard it too, but in one more second, carrying her glass steadily, she had edged through the crowd to Hubert's side. "Here," she said.

"I thought you had died," said Hubert. "Some darn fool has turned in an alarm."

He took the glass and emptied it over the hole from which the smoke was coming. There was a hiss and the smoke began to smell dead, and then thinned out to nothing.

"Shall I get another?" asked Edie.

"Sure," said Hubert. "We might as well do a good job."

This time she had a hard time setting out as the crowd around them was three feet deep, but it had moved back a little when someone said: "The dang thing's liable to blow up any time," so she was able to wriggle through. While she was gone, Hubert opened the Ford's back door, pulled out the mashed box of kitchen matches, threw them into the gutter, and stamped on them.

"Lord, here they are," he said as Edie came back. "What'll we do now?"

"It's no use asking *me*," said Edie. "How did we get a fire anyhow?"

Hubert didn't answer as he threw the second glass of water onto the blackened mat and closed the door firmly.

The fire engines drew up, with a terrible clatter, and all the firemen except the driver got solemnly down. They didn't say anything, but prowled around the car and looked at the Cares from head to foot. The Chief in his hat, boots, coat, and with an ax in his hand finally confronted Hubert. "You kids turn in an alarm?" he asked.

"No," said Hubert.

"They was afire," said a voice from the crowd.

"What I want to know is, who turned in that alarm," said the Chief sternly, looking the crowd over.

"Not me," said Hubert. "Take the glass back. Hurry," he said to Edie.

When she got back this time, he was in the driver's seat with his foot and hand ready.

"Are we all right?" said Edie. "Here, Widge!"

"The beagle's traveling house got a little singed on the bottom," Hubert said out of the corner of his mouth as he put his foot down to throw in the gear, "but he's all right. I took a look. But he must have been plenty hot." He made the car go ahead just enough to part the crowd. They did not want to let them go. Someone wanted to investigate the cause of the fire, and someone else wanted to arrest them.

"I expect the eggs are cooked," said Hubert, nosing along. "We can have them for lunch."

"I don't want any lunch," said Edie.

As soon as the way was clear, he twitched his finger, and

the Ford gave a bound. They whistled out of town with all the windows open and their hair blowing. "Phew," said Hubert, "phew, phew, phew. Look, if you smell us so violently again, you might let me know sooner." He closed one eye and gave Edie a glance sideways.

"It wasn't my fault any more than yours," said Edie. "But what I'd like to know is, how did it get started and is it going to do it again?" She turned around and peered and sniffed.

"Positively not," said Hubert. "That I can assure you. As for getting started, you'll never know, you'll never, never know.

"And what I wonder," he added, giving Edie another glance, "is who turned in that fire alarm. Eh?"

"You'll never know," said Edie, "you'll just never, never know."

When they had left Grampham and were on nearly empty roads again, Hubert said they better hurry a bit they had lost so much time, so he twitched down his finger and things swam past. He also made the most of the straight stretches, and at Harland he said he knew a short cut round the town.

"I'll bet you don't really," said Edie encouragingly.

"Madam showed it to me," said Hubert. "Anyway I have a much better sense of direction than you do."

Edie opened and shut her mouth. "I don't mind going a hundred miles an hour," she said later. "But I do mind getting lost with this zoo on our hands." She turned round to try and comfort Jocko who was crying in little sniffs.

"Good Jock, good little Jock. Here nibble my finger awhile."
She was flung against Hubert as he rounded a corner. They
were off on his short cut.

"I don't remember this at all," she said as they came to a
heavily wooded place with a narrow road. But it was straight
and Hubert was whistling through his teeth with pleasure
and making the Ford tear down it.

"You'll see," he said complacently.

It did seem to be going in the right direction, and it was
an awfully nice road. It thinned and thickened so that sometimes you could see the chimneys of the town and sometimes you were in lonely woods. There were hardly any cars
on it. Maybe the old guy was right and knew what he was
talking about, Edie decided. They were certainly making
up lost time. In fact, they were going along at such a clip
that they did not see a man who popped out of the bushes
behind them and waved his arms. He was not waving to
them, however, but to someone down the road in front of
them, who also popped out from the bushes, stood in the
middle of the road, and made himself into a windmill.
When they were near enough, they saw that this was a policeman; he had on his pot helmet, blue coat with silver
buttons, boots, billy, and all. Hubert had to slow down, and
as the policeman jumped from side to side of the road, he
finally had to stop.

"You're a menace to this town," said the policeman in
a squeaky voice, shaking his billy at them. "You're a menace
to this town." He came round to the side of the car.

"What have I done?" said Hubert innocently.

"You've exceeded the speed limit. It's twenty miles an hour. You was goin' fifty."

"Nonsense!" said Hubert.

"You were," said Edie.

"You keep your mouth shut," said Hubert softly. "It's a police trap. Look over there."

There was a clearing in the woods to the right and Edie could hardly believe it, but it was full of policemen all in their pot helmets and uniforms, sitting in chairs in the shade of the trees. There was a table in front of them and another man without a uniform was sitting there with papers laid out that he was studying.

"You're arrested," said the one by the car. "Get out of that there automobile, young feller. You'll have to come before the judge."

"All right," said Hubert amiably. "Where is he?"

He was the man at the table. It was all exactly like Robin Hood, Edie thought, but they were treating Hubert as if he were a fat abbot and not Will Scarlet. They made him stand and be judged, and then he had to pay ten dollars for going too fast. The policemen in the chairs all leaned forward eagerly when he took out the money, and he did it so slowly and carefully that Edie wondered for a minute if he were going to jump and run. She got ready. But Hubert put the ten dollars on the table.

"A receipt, if you don't mind," he said to the judge.

The judge narrowed his eyes at him. "Don't get fresh with me, you young squirt," he said. "I'm the law. We're going to stamp out you speeders if we die in the attempt."

"Get 'em back in their flivver," he said to the policeman who had stopped them.

The policeman did it by guiding Hubert by the seat of his pants with his billy. As Hubert bent over to get in, he gave him an extra hard tap. Edie could have told him it wasn't exactly the thing to do. Hubert seldom got mad, but when he did, there was a lot of smashing and whacking for miles around. This time his face got red and his neck and even his ears. Edie thought she saw the hair on the back of his neck standing up like a dog's. She was scared.

"Let's get out of here," she said, as she shut the car door.

"Just a minute, just a minute," said Hubert. "Don't be in such a hurry. There's something I have to do." He stretched himself all over and loosened his collar and took some long breaths before he started the Ford. Slowly and carefully he crept down the road for about a hundred yards.

"Take a look behind," he said to Edie. "The robbers! Are they still out on the road?"

"Nope," said Edie. "They're counting their money I guess." What was he going to do for heaven's sake? She hoped that getting mad hadn't "turned his brain," the way Nurse used to say it could. But, of course, it had.

Hubert put on all the speed he could, and they tore away from the police trap making mountainous clouds of dust. The wind certainly blew it to settle right on the policemen, and behind its fog and just before the end of the long straight stretch he turned round. They raced back, skipping and bouncing on the uneven road. Before they got really in sight of the trap he slowed down. Two policemen were standing in the road this time. Hubert crawled up to them and past them and away from them keeping the law perfectly. He lifted one hand and nicked his head to them and to the judge over in the bushes with the greatest politeness. "'Do, Officer," he said, "'do, Judge."

"We'll go by once more," he said, turning. "As a matter of fact we have to, to finish the short cut."

"Well, the animals don't like it," said Edie. "And I don't either. But I suppose you're crazy and we'll have to stand it."

"Good guess," said Hubert. "This is something like," he added.

"Maybe it is," said Edie, "but only for one single person."

Hubert didn't answer because he was concentrating on just the right time for him to slow up. There were four policemen in the road this time. They thought they could block him of course, but he would quietly and dignifiedly go round them at fifteen miles an hour. He put on the brakes quite hard to stop in time, and their dust began catching up with them, the policemen, and the judge as well. It made Jocko sneeze and the troupial cough, and the beagle way down below made retching sounds in his throat. But these were all drowned out by a loud report. The Ford swerved and swiveled, but Hubert managed to keep it on the road while it began to bump and grind like an old tip cart.

"Gee, look!" said Edie, sitting up and staring.

"Cripes!" said Hubert, taking a fast peek, while he was trying to pull over and stop the car.

One of the back tires, collapsing from the puncture, had

come off and was spinning along first beside, and then ahead, going right straight for the judge. While the Ford quivered and stood still almost pressed against the stomachs of the four policemen, Hubert as well as Edie watched with their stomachs nearly up to their mouths. The tire couldn't have been happier; it bounced over stones, jumped ruts, kicked up straws, and never lost a bit of speed. Until it hit the table. That was the terrible moment. Would it come down on the judge's head and brain him or would it fall round him like a doughnut, or would it glance off and land in the laps of the other policemen? Edie shoved back on the seat as the tire bumped and went up in the air. When it fell dead at the foot of the table, whirling round and round like a dog settling down, she let out her breath. Hubert heard her.

"You don't need to be so relieved," he said. "That's only the beginning."

It certainly was. They were surrounded without a minute's delay by the whole force, who took the Ford and propelled it by hand to the side of the road. They then invited Hubert and Edie to step out a second time. The judge waved them to chairs at the side of the table and picked up the receiver of the telephone that was hanging beside him on a tree. He rang the bell violently.

"It's the jug for you," he said as he waited for the operator.

It looked as if it were going to be, because when he got the number he wanted, he told the station to send the wagon right over.

"Is that the Black Maria?" said Edie, whispering. She had

her arms around Widgy whose tongue was dripping all over the table.

"Kindly move that animal," said the judge when he sat down again. "Now, young man, I'll thank you to answer a few questions. As you will certainly spend the night in jail, I shall have to know what to do with your sister here." He paused. "She is your sister, I take it? Or is this a case of kidnaping too?"

Hubert was sitting with his chin in his hands and did not answer. At first he had been looking at nothing except the fact that he was ruined forever. Somebody would certainly come and take care of Edie and the animals; they might even get him out of jail after a while, though he wasn't so sure of that; but what he was sure of was that he would never be allowed to use the car again. It was one of the gloomiest thoughts he had ever had and hard to tear himself away from. Then, suddenly, he was torn away in spite of himself. Far, far, down the road there was a speck; there was lots of dust behind it and it was bowling along like anything. One of the officers saw it too and craned forward eagerly. They were going to hold up somebody else!

"Speak up!" said the judge.

"She *is* my sister," said Hubert, sitting up. The oncoming car was almost in plain sight. He leaned forward. Sure as shooting—there was the man up the road waving his arms as a signal and an officer had stepped out in front of them here.

"Quite a haul today," said the judge, pleased, as he looked too.

He was too interested to go on with the proceedings for

a minute. He and Hubert watched the car come on at a great rate.

"Edie," said Hubert suddenly, very quietly. "Take a look."

Edie raised her eyes above Widgy's head. Oh no! There were Father and Madam and the three maids and the children in the Packard hurtling into the police trap. Both Cares jumped to their feet and yelled at the top of their lungs. "Look out! LOOK OUT!" Their shouts didn't do the least good. In another two minutes Father was being arrested like anybody else. Well, it was rather a relief; to Hubert anyway. At least the family would know what jail he had been taken to and also—Hubert's insides were lit by a beautiful light for a moment—under the circumstances what could Father say! He felt very much like smiling—but didn't—until right on the Packard's heels came the Black Maria.

"The Lord keep us and save us," said Cook from the back of the Packard excitedly, as she saw it. "They have us lynched."

"'Tis pinched you mean," said Gander. "L'ave you be quiet now till the Master talks to the gentlemen."

"Pinched or lynched," said Cook hysterically, "I'll go no place in that thing."

Madam had to turn round and put her hand on her knee; The Fair Christine and Lou were struggling to get out from behind the elbow barricade and be hysterical too. "Sh," she said. "Of course not. Mr. Cares will take care of it."

The new girl, whose hair had gotten away from the yachting cap and veil, said her prayers.

It seemed to take a long time for Mr. Cares to take care of it. He could pay his own fine and go along if he liked, but they had got hold of a criminal like Hubert and they did not mean to let him go. They were going to teach him a lesson and, besides, he was in contempt of court. Two officers were now on either side of him and one of them had taken out a pair of handcuffs.

"He'll go quietly, I'm sure," said Father. "But hold on a minute."

Hubert had never known he was such a wonderful character until Father got through talking. He was indispensable at home, he was a stunner at school, he was a genius with cars and animals, and finally his respect and consideration for the police until this moment had been profound. His only fault, he discovered, was that he sometimes was up to boyish pranks.

"I'd almost rather be arrested," he said to Edie under his breath.

"How's that?" said Father sharply.

"I just said I was sorry, sir," said Hubert meekly.

Madam finally saved the day as usual. She got out of the car with all her veils floating round her and came up to the table. "Your Honor," she said, "this is my only son." Good heavens, she sounded just like the Bible. Hubert hoped he was not that bad. "Up until today his conduct has been exemplary. Perhaps there was something—" Madam looked around at the Force, who sat like frogs ready to stick out their sticky tongues. Like frogs you couldn't tell a thing from looking at their faces. Madam tried again, because when she looked at the judge, he looked at the table. He might be weakening. "I really think there must have been—"

Edie stepped up to the table and put Widgy down on it. "He hit 'im," she said.

"Who?" asked Madam.

"A police officer struck a child!" said Father.

Edie pointed him out, and the policeman immediately took off his helmet and mopped his brow. "I give him a tap," he said.

"It was a good hard whack," said Edie. It was so seldom safe and good at the same time to tell the truth that she thought she might as well make the most of it.

"Are you hurt, my boy?" Father asked Hubert.

Hubert wriggled his shoulders to try out his back. "It will probably stiffen up later on," he said.

The judge looked from one Cares to the other, and there was quite a long silence while he must have been making up his mind.

"Mr. Cares," he said finally. "It seems apparent that both your family and mine have been in error. I shall be obliged to punish them both. Sergeant Crotty"—he turned to the policeman who had given Hubert the tap—"you can go back to the station in the wagon and stay there for the day. Mr. Cares, twenty-five dollars, please. Ten is your own fine. Fifteen is bail for your son—"

"No," said Father firmly, "no bail."

"Fifteen is your son's fine for rudeness, contempt, bad behavior, and discomfiture of public officials." He brushed clouds of dust from his suit so that they could all see it.

"You hear that, Hubert?" said Father. He paid over the money, counting it out slowly, and the judge gathered it up and put it in a strong box on the table at his right hand.

"To be used for the apprehension of speeders," he said tightly. "Good day, sir."

The minute they got away Hubert was dying of hunger again. He had used up Nurse's sausages and ice cream on the police trap, he said. Putting on the tire he had had to accomplish like a camel by using his hump.

"You mean the one the policeman hit?" said Edie.

He was forced to get hold of her braid and pull it till she apologized.

This did not solve the hunger question. They had a perfectly good basket packed by Gander and Cook with a lot of things in it that Hubert himself had recommended, but Edie said they had to find a decent place to eat it in. She wanted trees, or a hill, or a brook; she didn't want to eat with road dust falling on everything. She'd had enough of that already thanks to—

"You know what's the matter with you, don't you?" said Hubert. "You're starving yourself."

She finally let him stop when they were just outside Mansett. There was a thread of cool breeze by that time, just a thread, bringing the sea, and yet it somehow went all over you like salt water. The daisy fields of the middle country had been left behind. Now it was mostly scrub pine and little oaks, but they found a grove of them a little way from the road.

"The animals must need a rest too," said Edie.

"We'll take them all out," said Hubert, "and give 'em a treat."

"What kind of a treat?" Edie asked suspiciously as she was carrying Jocko to the trees.

"Oh, a little liberty," said Hubert airily.

"Hubert," said Edie, "if you let one of these animals out of its cage, I'll—" She could not think of any threat bad enough, but she *did* think that looking after a man was the hardest work you could do in a dog's age.

But after lunch, and after the animals' lunch, Hubert said he hadn't the strength of a flea. He lay on his back and patted his stomach. "It would be nice if there were a fire somewhere," he said, "just for a little excitement."

"And several people roasted, I suppose," said Edie.

"I wouldn't go as far as that," said Hubert. "Just a baby or two thrown out the window."

He did not exactly go to sleep, but he took a rest with his eyes closed and what Edie thought was a very sinister look on his face, that is, half smiling to think how wonderful he was. She stayed near the cages and did not shut an eye.

Still, she could not possibly blame him for what happened next. When they were on the road again, he drove as sedately as a grandmother. He kept saying he was being suffocated; he loosened his tie to show her his sufferings, but he did not speed; he did not even go fast enough so that the smell blew backwards. If there were a party of hens in the road, he practically stopped until they had all gone shrieking to one side or the other, and with horses he did stop and ask the men who owned them if he could help. This was hard on his politeness because the men swore at him just the same.

"You're being awfully proper," said Edie rashly.

Hubert said nothing until he had taken out a cigarette and lit it right under her nose. He could do it with one hand by cracking the match with his fingernail.

"Have you forgotten, my good woman, that our respected parent may be behind us. They were all stopping at Bay's Landing, remember, to show off the kids to that friend of Father's."

"What *I'd* like to do most is cool off my feet."

"If they're that hot, I'd rather have them out than in," said Hubert, "so go ahead."

Edie fixed herself comfortably by leaning against him with her feet over the door until he unexpectedly leaned forward and jogged her up too. They had reached Barnet Bay, where the road ran along by the shore for a while, and the cool, damp air was delicious. All her insides had begun to dance around at the thought of the sea. Tomorrow she might be in it. Tonight she might even be able to go out and polish brass on one of the boats. She didn't like being disturbed in the middle of such good thoughts.

"What's the matter now?" she said.

"Do you know what that is?" said Hubert, stabbing his finger at some rolls of cotton wool low down on the horizon.

"Yup," said Edie. "Fog."

Hubert reached into the back without taking his eyes off the road and pulled out an alarm clock. "Pretty good in one try," he said. "It is now a quarter past three. At four o'clock we ought to be turning in the avenue at Aunt Louise's. The fog doesn't usually come in until five, but it looks awfully close today."

"What do we care," said Edie. "We're on dry land."

Hubert just took to whistling through his teeth.

They met the fog, or rather, it met them at a quarter of four as they were going through a long stretch of scrub land beyond Barnet. They did not see it coming, or dive into it. The day gradually got gloomy, that was all, and Hubert had to keep getting out to wipe the windshield. Very soon he was driving with his head out the side window and the door a little open. The animals, he said, would have to take it or leave it; he had never seen it so thick in his life.

Presently no matter what Hubert did he could hardly see where they were going. He tried lighting the headlights. At any rate, he explained, it would be a good thing not to get hit in the rear, especially not by Father. This made him open his mouth and laugh silently, but all the time he was wriggling in his seat and peering with all his might, and so was Edie. This road through the scrub was small and winding and lots of other roads ran off from it. It was a relief when they ran again into the moorlike country that on clear days gave a view all the way down to the beaches and the sea. Just now the only way they knew it was there was because the air had become a little lighter. Hubert made Edie get out and feel the brush at the side of the road. She disappeared a yard from the running board. "Come back," he called.

"I'm right here," said Edie with her face almost in the

car. She and Widgy got in together. "It's the Mount Harbor road all right," she said. "At least I think it is."

"What does the brush feel like?"

"Stiff and prickly and about two feet high."

"It sounds right," said Hubert.

He waited a minute with the mist all around them thick and white. They could see the road at their feet if they stared; everything else was shut away. Hubert shut off the lights; they only reflected back and made things worse. He felt sure they couldn't be far now from Mount Harbor, but for all he could really tell, they might be on the moon. In fact, it felt very much like the moon. Or they might have turned round and be going back to Summerton. Fog did some pretty funny things to you. He started the car again, however. "We can't stay here," he said. "I wonder why there's no traffic."

They had thought they knew every inch of the way, every turn of the road and curve of the shore, but the fog took away even the memory of how things were. Hubert could only keep his eyes fixed on a spot that looked like the crown of the dirt road. Edie was looking for the turn that went to Aunt Louise's. If they didn't make it, they would be off down the beach for miles and miles. Mount Harbor was the last town until you got to Melboro at the end of the beach altogether. They jerked along for what seemed at least an hour. Where the dickens was Mount Harbor itself?

"You've missed it," said Hubert suddenly accusingly.

Edie looked at the clock. "According to you it isn't time yet."

"According to me it's *more* than time."

Their voices had become serious and quiet, their faces and hair were dripping, and Edie's cotton dress clung around her. But she was very alive inside it, trying to see through the fog by sheer will power. When the road began to get bumpy, however, she sat back holding Widgy, as still as a mouse.

"This must be the avenue," said Hubert.

"We haven't gone through Mount Harbor yet," said Edie into Widgy's hair.

Hubert paid no attention, but bumped along regardless. "Aunt Louise ought to have this road fixed," he said, annoyed.

Just after this the bumping stopped, the front wheels slewed a little, the back wheels settled down, and the car stalled. For a minute there was absolute silence except for Laza's hopping. Through it presently they could hear the tiny lap and swish of water on a beach. Edie jumped down into sand. That's where they were—on a beach. She picked up some sand and dribbled it before Hubert's eyes.

"Oh for the love of Jehosephat!" said Hubert. "How did we get here? And where is it?"

They stood next to each other in front of the Ford and looked from side to side. It was perfectly nice and clean and decent, but blind. Ahead of them was still the lap and swish that must be part of the sea, but they couldn't see it. They went backwards toward it, carefully keeping the black lump of the car in their eyes, and almost wet their sneakers it was so near.

"Well," said Hubert, sounding quite pleased, "we *are* in a fix. Let's go swimming."

"And get lost in the ocean," said Edie. "No thanks."

Hubert thought they could take care of that by putting the alarm clock on the radiator of the car and setting it for five minutes from now.

"And if that's not enough for you, you stay on the beach while I go in and I'll stay while you go. We can yell at each other."

Widgy was already sitting at the edge of the water looking as if he could see through the fog way out to Spain.

Hubert's idea worked perfectly. The alarm clock went off making a terrible noise and guiding him safely back to shore. He generously gave Edie ten minutes and did himself up in a comforter Madam had put over Laza at the last minute. She conversed with him from behind the white curtain. It was lonely out there when all you could see was yourself. Besides, she kept hearing things. She told Hubert so when she came in. He gave her the comforter and went out and listened.

"You certainly do," he called to her from the water.

"What *is* it?" said Edie, shivering a little.

They had been long enough in the fog for everything to seem queer. It was queer just listening to Hubert behind the white veil.

"It's voices," he said. "I'm going to see. Keep letting off the alarm clock, and for goodness sake don't lose your hearing or your voice." She could hear him flapping and splashing and then diving back into the water. "Edie," he called when he came up, "can you hear me? Use the car horn once in a while. Did you hear?"

"YES!" yelled Edie, till her voice almost split.

Hubert had some wonderful ideas sometimes, she had to acknowledge, but at the moment she was hating him. And she was hating every single boy in the world. Look at the poor fool going out to get lost in the Atlantic Ocean. It would serve him right if he drowned. It would serve him right if a shark got him. There weren't any sharks at the beach, her mind said. All right, she would make one. All the time she was walking back to the car to blow the horn she was so mad at Hubert that she was killing him off right and left, but when she got back to the beach and heard nothing, even though she called and called, she began to worry. Hubert was lost at sea, that was sure. And those noises, what were they? She became so anxious she began to forget her good sense and took a step into the water and then went farther and farther out, calling louder and louder and more and more furiously. She would pretty soon have to begin to swim. The water was up to her chest when something bumped her from the back. "OOOPS," she said, jumping, her heart almost stopping. A spook had her! She was so far in the water that it took a long time to turn, and Widgy came round in front. The sight of him splashing and panting brought her back from the land of spooks. She couldn't take *him* along. "*You* can't come," she said. "You go on back." She waved him toward what she thought was the shore and then realized that with her twisting and turning she had lost it. There was no car, no beach, nothing but the white veil. "Now I've done it," she thought, trying to steady herself to think what to do next. The tips of her toes were still on the bottom. That knowledge came to her like a drink of fresh, cold water. Maybe Widgy could help too, although right now he was trying to cling round her neck like a drowning sailor. She turned him round and started him swimming and then very, very slowly moved her toes forward, while she pushed the water back, to see if they would go uphill. Widgy tried to come back. "Bad dog," she said. "Go home!" Reluctantly he turned again. He might be right, but she still couldn't feel whether she were going uphill or down with her feet. A feeling so bad and terrible began to come at her that she thought it might kill her right there. She began to talk to Widgy loud and fast. "Good dog," she said as if she were telling him to get a rat. "Good dog, find the shore, that's a dandy dog. Hurry, Widgy, hurry." The sound of her voice so longing and so nice turned Widgy back of course, but by that time it did not matter. She found that she was able to set down one foot flat on the ocean bottom and still be chest high out of the water. She *must* be going uphill. In a second more she was at the water's edge and in another few steps she could see the car. All this time Hubert had been without any direction finder! She ran. And for the next three minutes she set off one thing after the other—clock and horn. She followed them by going down to the beach and standing just out of reach of the water yelling: "HUBERT!" at the top of her lungs, leaning out into the mist.

"Shut up," said Hubert's face right in front of her, and he came stalking out of the water with a rope over his shoulder. Edie could not decide if he looked more like something out of the Bible or out of a fairy book. She backed up in front of him. "Where *have* you been? What have you *got?*"

"A—Great—Big—Fish," said Hubert, pulling a boat into sight.

Of all the sights she ever saw in her life! In the boat were three maids, well maybe one was a cook, in their uniforms with their caps on their heads and their aprons on. And they were all dying of some kind of—well, what was it? Probably embarrassment, because the maids in the stern had their heads down and their faces were bright red, and the cook in the middle had her head up and she was almost purple. She, Edie saw, had oars in her hands. Hubert pulled them in as far as the load would go up the beach.

"May I assist you?" he said to the cook, holding out his hand at the bow.

Edie would certainly have liked to know how Hubert got so wonderful all of a sudden, but she would have liked too to give him a little advice. That really wasn't the thing to say to that cook. She was too fat. If Hubert had assisted her, she might have squashed him flat, but she had the good sense to get over the side about amidships by herself—into a little water but never mind that. The maids, who were thin, took his hand and jumped down to dry land. They each made him a little curtsy. "Thank you kindly, sir," they said. Then like two sandpipers and a gull they all went off up the beach.

"Hey," said Edie, "they'll get lost, won't they?"

"Do you know where we are?" said Hubert solemnly, watching the maids. "We're on the Waldrons' beach just before Mount Harbor. We've been down that road a hundred times. Right *there*," he said, pointing into the fog, "is the Waldrons' pier. You can go over and look if you want. And right there"—he pointed in the other direction—"is that big rock where they have picnics. Go and look, go and look."

"I believe you," said Edie, "but we're stuck just the same."

"They're going to send some men and a horse," said Hubert. "All we need to do is get turned round; home's just round the corner."

"What happened to them?"

"Oh, they just went for a row on a sunny day," said Hubert. He tugged the boat as far up the beach as he was able to pull it with Edie's help. "But I don't *believe*," he added, "that that cook can row very well."

Edie and Hubert, in spite of all their delays, arrived at Aunt Louise's first. Instead of sending horses, Mrs. Waldron's maids sent three men who with Hubert picked the Ford up, turned it round, and set it on firm ground.

"The most remarkable performance ever perpetrated," Hubert said, as he again twitched the accelerator and rattled off.

"Well, you saved their lives," said Edie.

"Most people aren't so grateful," said Hubert wisely. "How about keeping your head out the window instead of your feet so we can tell where we're going."

Mount Harbor, misty and indistinct, showed up almost as soon as they had turned off their side road, and from there they counted the houses to Aunt Louise's turnoff, saying their inhabitants by name. They rattled over the railroad bridge at the beginning of her avenue and ran down the shell road. There it was, as misty and indistinct as the Mount Harbor houses, but wonderful, they thought, to have been found at last—a big wood and plaster house with ells, balconies, turrets, piazzas, and a cupola, sitting on a little bluff guarded by some gigantic pines and pressed upon by bayberry bushes that climbed up from the shore. When they stopped at the front door and Hubert had turned off the ignition, they were again enveloped in the silence and loneliness of the fog. They sat there a minute listening to it and stretching.

"What was our hurry," said Hubert finally. "No cook, no food, no family."

"The key's under the first log in the wood pile by the kitchen door. Madam said so," said Edie.

"Get it," said Hubert. "I'll take out the animals. I hope they're still alive. I haven't heard a croak from that blamed bird since we were at lunch."

While Edie was gone, he decorated Aunt Louise's steps with the contents of the Ford. Laza was all right, but he was glaring with rage and opening his bill ready to snap off anybody's finger who dared to come near. The goat had his mouth open too, and also Father's beagle, who was panting. Jocko was crouched in a corner of his small traveling cage looking sad and wilted.

"They all need water," said Hubert when Edie came back.

"It isn't there," said Edie.

"Go get some."

"I said it wasn't there."

"What? Water?"

"No, the key."

"Blast!" said Hubert, who had got as far as the ice-cream freezer and was trying to tug it out from between the egg and butter container and some pots and pans.

"I'd get some from the garden faucet, but what in?" said Edie obligingly.

"Here, take this saucepan."

The garden was on the other side of a tiny wood above the railroad tracks, and it did not take her long. They let the beagle have the first drink, and he lapped until the saucepan was entirely empty so that she had to go for more. Then it was the goat's turn, but he would not drink except from his bottle, and that had to be found among the mess on the steps. He took three bottles before he started chewing the nipple, and Hubert had had time to bravely hook out Laza's drinking cups with one finger and fill them.

"Now Jock," said Edie.

"You better put it in his cage," said Hubert.

"Oh, why?" said Edie. "The poor thing. Anyway the saucepan's too big." She opened Jock's cage and coaxed him to come to the door. He looked at her and at the saucepan, bewildered. Then he tried to lift it up, but it was too heavy for him.

"He wants something smaller," said Hubert. "Try this measuring cup."

Jocko politely and carefully drank out of the measuring cup, and when he was through, handed it back to Edie.

"Good little monk," said Edie.

As she put out her hand to take the cup, Jock pulled her fingers as he often did with his cool dry hand and Edie let him have them. But this time he pulled harder than usual, and then he pulled her arm with all four paws as he ran up it to her shoulder, jumped off to the ice-cream freezer, to the top of Laza's cage, to the ground, and was across the side lawn in a twinkling and halfway up one of Aunt Louise's giant pines before they had time to start after him. They could not see him, but they could hear him chattering with pleasure.

"Bright girl," said Hubert. "I suppose you know just exactly what to do now, especially," he added, "as I see his royal highness approaching down the drive."

Edie looked. He was right. Down the shell road was chugging Mount Harbor's old only cab and Jane was looking out its window. Inside were certainly Theodore and that Miss Black they had been sent to meet.

"*I* couldn't help it," said Edie.

This, however, was not Theodore's point of view at all. As soon as he was told, it was quite clear, he said, that they had made a stupendous mess of things. "And I don't mean what's on the steps," he said. Jane had to pay the cab and get out the bags and stand beside the square light-haired woman who was Miss Black while he told them this and they told him they would be highly pleased if he would just shut up.

"Have you tried the door?" Theodore asked in the end.

Hubert and Edie agreed later that it was something they would probably never get over till the end of their lives that Aunt Louise's front door was not locked and Ted got in as easy as silk. They could have taken all the animals in and made them comfortable and never have lost Jocko at all. It made them blush to think of it.

In the hall Jane tried to introduce Miss Black, but by then no one could pay attention. They were ordered at once to take part in Jocko's capture.

"We can only get him from the roof," said Theodore. "And we'll have to let out that bird and use his cage. It's a lot bigger than Jock's traveler. We can catch the bird later. Bring the eggs," he said to Hubert. "We'll try him with those."

"I've got an apple left from lunch," said Edie.

"Bring that," said Theodore.

For some reason "unknown to man" as Hubert said afterwards, Laza was brought upstairs and let out in the room that Father and Madam usually had when they were at Aunt Louise's, and Theodore—carrying eggs, apple and cage—went up the stairs and through the trap door to the roof, where one of the pines rested a branch on the top of the piazza. Everyone else stood and looked at each other and waited. They couldn't go with Theodore for fear of scaring Jocko, and they didn't want to go away for fear of missing some excitement. They were not thinking of Miss Black when she came up and joined them.

"Oh, I forgot," said Jane. "This is Miss Black. Edie—Hubert."

"Jeananne," said Miss Black. "We are going to be great friends, Edie and I." She put her arm around Edie's shoulders. "And Hubert too, I am sure." They had to try to smile at her while they were listening hard for Ted. "And now wouldn't it be nice and also polite if you were to bring up the bags, Hubert. Your sister and I are all smuts from the train."

"Just a sec," said Hubert, cocking his head for Ted's dulcet tones with Jocko.

"And Edith too," she went on, "had better get ready for her father and mother."

"My stepmother," said Edie. "And I *am* ready. Would you mind not talking for half a minute? We want to hear—"

"Oh no, dear," said Miss Black, "we must change, you know, when we're untidy. Let's give your parents a surprise."

Edie had managed to wriggle out from under the arm and Hubert had gone to the cupola stairs to hear better when Ted at last came neatly down with Jocko in Laza's cage. Jocko was sucking an egg. There was a good deal of egg everywhere, they noticed. But Ted was pleased. "Got him," he said. "The eggs did it. I had to use about six, though. Jane you go get his traveler. We'll put him in it for now and you kids help me clean this out so we can get that bird back."

Miss Black was left standing in the hall while Hubert and Edie trailed after Theodore to the basement and the laundry tubs. It was she who had to welcome the Packard when it came and she who, unfortunately, did not know where Laza had been allowed his freedom, so that when Father brought up the first bags and opened the door, they met face to face, and Laza was so furious he bit him on the nose.

After that, as Theodore remarked, "How could pandemonium go further?"

Madam, as usual, straightened things out and got everybody and everything into their proper places and Father's nose repaired. Luckily it was not a deep peck and only bled like a shaving wound, persistently, but not badly. Besides, she claimed that Laza was her bird and so it was all her fault.

She shooed Cook into the kitchen to put on the kettle and Gander upstairs to change so that she could get tea right away. She showed them both that their supplies were on the kitchen steps in market baskets. She handed the children over to Miss Black and showed her what rooms to use, and then she threw her veil way back, took off her hat, and went in and caught Laza barehanded.

"What a woman!" said Theodore, as they were taking the other animals up to the old barn where Jocko was to have the pigeon loft and Billy Whiskers, the goat, a box stall.

"Just my sentiments," said Hubert. "But it's a pity she can't lay eggs."

"He's trying to be funny again," said Theodore to Jane.

"I was never more serious in my life," said Hubert. "We *may* get dinner, if Cook feels up to it, but I looked in the egg box after you and Jocko got through, and I should say that for breakfast there's about half an egg apiece."

CHAPTER TWO

Terrible, Horrible Edie

In the summer, at the beach, there were the three best smells in the world, Edie thought, and she was smelling them—hot piazza boards, honeysuckle, and wild roses. She sniffed at her brown arms. Even she herself smelled pretty good. She loved this place, she loved it so much that she hardly minded having to stay on the balcony of Aunt Louise's boathouse because she was in exile. She simply enjoyed snuffing it in. As for those older kids and people, if they wanted to be unfair, let them. Never in her ten years long of life had she ever known Theodore or Jane or Hubert to do a kind act, and now that they considered themselves as old as Methuselah, what could she do against them? Naturally they sided with "G-nan" Black who was as ancient as they were. She might have known that as soon as Father and Madam went away, leaving a policewoman to rule over her, they would all want to shut her up. As for Susan Stoningham, who, after Widgy, used to be her best friend, Edie did not even want to think about her any more. She had turned out to be a traitor, a *real* traitor, who not only was willing to go back on a friend, but also on her country, the United States of America.

"Widgy," said Edie, "come here, good dog."

Widgy swiggled over on his baking stomach and put his chin on the back of her knee.

It was because of this traitorousness that Edie had got into trouble. She had had to fight Susan on the Main Street of Mount Harbor, Massachusetts, just as people were going for their morning mail. Susan had been reading *The Little Colonel*. In fact, she had gotten up early in order to get it first and had hidden it in the bookcase so that she could sneak off with it after breakfast. (G-nan, the policewoman, had complimented her on tidiness, ha, ha!) But after all, that wasn't so bad, Edie acknowledged; she might have done that herself. What Susan did do was say out loud on the Main Street without any excuse except that her grandfather lived in Cambridge, Maryland, that she was for the South.

"Do you want slaves?" Edie had asked, shocked.

"I wouldn't mind a slave or two," said Susan carelessly.

"Well, the South got beaten, so you can't have them," said Edie, turning to walk backwards so she could see how Susan liked that.

"The Southerners were a lot better-looking anyway," said Susan, pushing her hair back.

"Not than Abraham Lincoln," said Edie quickly.

"That ol' Abe Lincoln," Susan had said, putting her hand over her mouth as if she would explode and talking as much like Cambridge, Maryland, as she could. "He looked just like a—"

Edie had given her a push. She staggered—she was fatter than Edie—but she did not fall down, and she kept right on talking like a traitor. She was glad "ol' Abe Lincoln the Ape" was dead. "The South, the South, the South," Susan kept saying louder and louder. She got her balance back and pushed Edie hard. Edie sat down, but only for a second, and she did her best to pull Susan's dress off.

"The North," she said breathlessly, "the North, the North." It was just when they had begun moving round each other to see who could get a punch in first that Mr. Archie Streeter interfered. He walked them back to Aunt Louise's with a hand on each of their shoulders. He was going their way, he said. And he did not have the tact to let them go at the beginning of the shell drive but kept them under his bony fingers all the way to the mulberry tree until he saw every single person they knew in this part of the country coming along—G-nan, all the rest of the family, even The Fair Christine and Lou. They had just thought of going for the mail themselves probably.

"Here come the Devil's Disciples," Theodore had said the minute he saw them.

Susan had thought it was funny, but Edie thought it was insulting. It was meant to be insulting, she was sure of that. Anyway it was just the kind of remark to start another fight, and Edie was just ready for it. She could not beat Theodore, but since she had grown her nails on purpose, she could nick a bit out of him here and there. Of course the policewoman thought she must protect him. She had taken Edie by the back of the pinafore and before them all made her walk to the boathouse. The pinafore had been like a strait jacket, and Edie had not been able to turn or even swing her arms. She tried to fall down, but that was impossible too. She tried to stop, but that awful great hand propelled her on.

"Take your hand off me and I will go myself," she said from the bottom of her throat.

"No," said the gorilla.

"I will promise you to go myself."

"No."

This was unheard of. Even Father took your promises. The gorilla was pushing her almost faster than she could walk so that she was up on her toes like a clown. She knew what they were doing and thinking behind her to see such a spectacle, but she hoped they realized she would never, never, never get over their letting her be hauled off like this when all she had done was try to stand up for her country.

At the boathouse the gorilla opened the door, pushed her in as if she were a wheel chair, slammed the door again, and locked it.

"Until you cool off," she had called as if she were God and owned the world.

There was no way to get out of the top of Aunt Louise's boathouse, everybody knew that, so Edie had gone to the balcony and lain down. She had spent a long time hating and despising G-nan. And lots of other people too. Susan, naturally, she said to herself sarcastically, being a guest, had gone off with them all to the village and was probably having an ice cream this minute. Seeing them all on the Mount Harbor Main Street where she and Susan had had the fight made her hurriedly feel in her pinafore pocket. Thank heavens, the fifty cents was still there. What a miracle after all that jouncing! She and Susan had been on the way to buy gear for the dory. There was a race this afternoon—not dories—but twenty-one footers and Theodore was taking out Cousin Blade's boat. They had meant to go and watch, and the dory needed some things; a rudder rope for one, a couple of reef ties, and some chocks because the mast was a little loose. Edie lifted her head and peeked through the balcony railing to the harbor. Three people were getting their boats ready, but there were more than that bobbing unused. It was too early. There was nothing that looked so unused as a boat when it wasn't doing anything. It was pathetic. She rolled over on her back and Widgy accommodatingly settled his head on her ankle, but the tip of his tongue touched her skin.

"Get off, I'm hot, you tickle," said Edie, twitching her leg so that Widgy flung himself panting in what shade there was.

She seemed to have been there now an awfully long time. She was suddenly too hot, too uncomfortable, and too alone. She wished she were in the house. If you couldn't always get piazza boards, honeysuckle, and roses to smell, Aunt Louise's house was almost as good. On good days all the big open high-ceilinged rooms were filled with a kind of sunny air that smelled of tea and pine needles, and on bad days, when everything was shut up, you were shut in with fog and the smell of a ship. It was delicious. How did Aunt Louise ever leave such a place? Her broad staircase went up by several landings to the second and third floors. Wind flapped the curtains in the mornings and blew them straight out in the afternoons. Doors slammed. As you lay in bed, you could hear boats chunking on the harbor water and see shadows flickering on the ceiling. Aunt Louise's chintz sitting-room had a great window seat flung out so far you felt you were on the lawn, and the room opposite across the hall, with wicker chairs, had red cushions. All of the piled cushions in both rooms smelt of mold. The big dining-room was hung with Cousin Blade's racing flags, and its view over the bayberry bushes was of the harbor—end to end. But what made Aunt Louise's especially good was that there was room for everybody. The Red House was a wonderful house, but it was getting crowded now that Madam was having more and more children. The Fair Christine and Lou were all right, of course, but they could sometimes make an awful mess. Here in Aunt Louise's they could do this on the top floor where nobody had to look at it, until, after several hundreds of years, as Theodore said, it got picked up. Edie had not liked Madam's children at first. Nobody had. They had only begun to when Chris was two years old and learned to stand on her head. Now that she was five, when you asked her to do a thing, she would do it. You hardly had to teach her. She could throw a ball or carry a glass, or put her food in her mouth without spilling it. And she looked quite respectable, Theodore and Hubert thought, like a picture of a girl in Edie's "First Reader." Lou was only three. Nobody ever tried asking her to do anything. Theodore considered her very good-looking and bright, but all she could do was give you a kiss whether you wanted it or not. She talked, but not straight. She called Edie, Mith-thes. It came from Mrs. Edith Cares, and *she* came out of a magazine Madam had been looking at. Nobody knew Mrs. Edith Cares and nobody wanted to, only Lou had to call Edie Mith-thes. "If you call that bright," Hubert had said shrugging his shoulders.

"Watch her," said Theodore, "she'll go far."

Edie was not cooling off, she was getting hotter and hotter, and she would probably starve to death anyway pretty soon, she was almost sure. G-nan would not mind that. Before Father and Madam had gone away, they had taken pains to get "a suitable person" to look after "the younger children." Aunt Charlotte had found Miss Jeananne Black and thought her terribly suitable to look after Chris and Lou. She said she was strong as a horse.

"Edith will also benefit," she had added.

Until this morning Edith had managed to stay away from being benefited. She had just minded her own business and let Miss Black mind hers with Chris and Lou. They didn't seem to mind her being superenormous.

"She is a horse and you never know when you might get stepped on," she had said to Hubert when they were scraping the skiff bottom.

"Maybe it wouldn't hurt you for once," Hubert had said callously.

The thing was that she didn't see how he could say a thing like that. The thing was that they had forgotten her and pretty soon it would be time for the boat race and she would not be ready. There must be some way to get out of this old place. She had just been waiting until she was told by her inside self to move. But in spite of wandering around, she had not found a way by the time there was a noise and she saw Susan, who must have climbed up the trellis by the front door, standing across the boathouse ridge pole looking down at her. She had a basket in her hand and she looked a

good deal like old Mr. Benjamin Bunny when he was looking for his son, but Edie was not feeling like laughing. She
threw herself down again and closed her eyes.

"Are you going to be good now?" Susan asked, grinning.

"Is she going to starve me to death?" asked Edie tightly.

"I've got your lunch with me. Do you want it now?"

"Yes," said Edie, "but not unless you'll take back about
Abraham Lincoln."

"All right," said Susan, "if you'll admit General Lee was
handsome."

"He might be handsome," said Edie, "but—"

"Ah, come on," said Susan, "don't start all over again."
She sat down and pulled a piece of string out of her pocket.

"I only got to bring you this," she said, still being quite
southern, "by thinking of everything. G-nan is afraid you'll
escape."

"Aren't they going to let me out of here?" asked Edie.

"Nope," said Susan, lowering the basket.

"Not for the race?"

"Nope."

"You mean—" said Edie, screwing up her face as if she
were looking into the sun. But what was the use of asking.
All of a sudden Edie's hand scrabbled in the basket of lunch
and began taking things out. She threw them with a jerk
over the balcony railings; the hard-boiled eggs splotched
against a tree, the orange rolled down the beach into the eelgrass, the bottle of milk broke on a rock.

"You'll be sorry," said Susan.

"Go away," said Edie. "I don't want you round any more."

"I'll come and see you when I get back," said Susan. "But I don't see any use of bringing anything if all you do is throw it away."

Edie didn't answer. She got up and went into the dark upper part of the boathouse where Aunt Louise kept a billiard table and a player piano and lay down there until she heard Susan pad along the roof and jump down into the hazel bushes. The trouble with *her* was that she was in love with Theodore. She thought he looked like a noble mountain goat. She didn't suppose there was any other man in the world who had reddish hair and reddish eyebrows too, she said.

"Don't forget he has green eyes," Edie had pointed out. And seeing that Susan was not impressed, she had added, "Anyway he's too bossy." But Susan had stuck to it; she liked to be bossed by a man. "That's because you haven't much of any in your family," said Edie. She thought perhaps she had better tell her that Ted called her "Sink 'em Susan" because she couldn't swim.

Edie sat up. She could see that she would be given food and drink if worse came to worst, but Susan was not going to do anything the noble goat would disapprove of, that was certain. Probably she would even sail in the race with him if he asked her. She had not known that there could be such treachery in the world. There must, must, must be some way to get out of here and fool them all. From the balcony it was too far to jump, and from the balcony railing the gutter was too high for her to reach and get on the roof; the honeysuckle vines here were weak things that had been affected by salt water—they wouldn't hold a baby. She got up and wandered around again. She couldn't use the billiard table or its black shiny cover. The walls were covered with flags. She couldn't use them; bunting always tore. When she got to the balcony door, she looked out over the harbor. It had sprung to life. White butterflies were fluttering everywhere. There were even some set to the wind, already out in the bay. She continued her circuit, entering the darkish room again and taking a look at the skylight. Even if she stood on the billiard table and a chair, she couldn't get up there. She opened cupboards. There was paint in one and a lot of old cleats in the other. Boo! Widgy panted after her and finally lay by the door where a little draft came in, watching her from between his paws.

"Why don't you help me, bad dog?"

Doing another round, she ran her hand along the walls. When she came to the door, she felt the panels. They were rather thin, like all doors at the beach. If she had something to break them with! But she did not really want to break Aunt Louise's door, so she went on and looked from the balcony once more. The boats had all flocked down to the harbor entrance and could just barely be seen on account of the pine trees. They would come in sight again as soon as they were out in the bay. The only one that was left was the Cares' dory, demasted and desolate right in front of her, tied to the float. It was a lumbering old thing compared with the P.D.Q., Cousin Blade's boat that Theodore was sailing, but she would know what to do with it if she could get out of here. Theodore had to admit she could sail, no matter what else was the matter with her.

Edie came round again to the tempting panels. They certainly were thin, and she had never seen so much light around the edge of a door before. It looked as if it had shrunk. Things shrank like anything at the beach. Her hand slid down to the handle. She would just try. She turned it and pulled. Nope, it was locked all right. She rattled it. Nope.

"Widgy, get out of the way!"

Edie gave the door a yank with her whole body attached to it, and the door opened so wide that she fell backwards. As soon as she walked out, she had to walk back again to shut up Widgy who had followed at her heels. "I can't take you," she said. "I would if I could, but you wouldn't like it anyway." She had to close the door carefully on account of his nose. "I *promise* to come back and get you," she said.

She was startled as she came out from the little ravine that ran down from the lawn to the beach. She had thought the place was deserted, but there right in front of her in the eelgrass were The Fair Christine and Lou. Chris had a rock in her hand, and they were looking concentratedly at the mud and gravel left by the low tide.

"What are you two doing?" said Edie. She certainly did not want them to think about *her*.

"We're persecuting crabs," said Chris.

"*What?*"

"We catch them and mash them," said Chris.

"What for?" said Edie sternly. "Don't you know you must never treat animals badly!" She took the rock away and threw it out in the water.

"They treated us badly," said Chris. "Anyway, Lou."

"Look, Mith-thes," said Lou.

She did have a small fiddler crab attached to her toe.

After Edie had taken it off, Lou gave her one of her hugs and kisses. It was just like eating a new doughnut while you put your face in sweet peas. But only Lou could do it. None of the other Cares knew how. Theodore and Hubert had often remarked on it. Edie would have liked to give her a treat in return, but what was there to do? Lou stood on one leg and held her other foot in her hand while she steadied herself on Edie.

"Mith-thes," she said, tipping her head so far back she almost upset, "would—you—take—us—out—on—the—ocean?"

Just by looking at Lou's face Edie got an idea that practically made her blind. Her ears sang, the top of her head burned.

"Where's G-nan?" said Edie hurriedly. She had expected her to be in hiding somewhere.

"She went to the bathroom," said Chris. "The tide's so low a flea couldn't get drowned. We're to stay right here." She paused. "But we didn't promise."

Edie started for the pier. The time was so short she was almost out of breath. "I *might* take you for a sail," she said, "if you come quick and do what I say." She dared to look toward the house. There was not a sign of anybody. Maybe G-nan had stopped to gossip with Gander.

The dory, as Edie had seen, was tied up to the float, but were the mast and rudder there? She hurried down the pier with the children trotting behind her. Yes, yes, *yes!* The first piece of luck she had had for a long time, she thought, forgetting the door that opened, being at Aunt Louise's, going sometimes as Theodore's crew when he sailed, getting driving lessons from Hubert on the back roads, swimming, fishing, sun, and all the good smells. Well, she was in a hurry. She had to step the mast, put on the rudder, fix the jib and centerboard, and get the kids into the boat before *any*body saw them, not just G-nan, but *any*body—because this was kidnaping and she knew it and she meant to do it. Besides having a marvelous time by turning up at the races and making them all goggle, she would practically kill G-nan in her tracks. G-nan would never, never, never dare to make a fool of her again.

Edie got the work done quickly. Theodore was right. She was a good sailor and she knew it too. She turned to look at the children. Chris was looking up at the house.

"I wonder if she's going to come," she said.

"I'm the captain of this boat now," said Edie, "and nobody matters but me. Get in."

Chris took a long precise step from the float to the middle of the dory's seat just as she was supposed to do. She settled herself neatly and quietly in the stern. Edie was puzzled for a minute, however, about what to do with Lou. She couldn't pull her in like a sack or roll her in like a barrel, and she was too heavy to lift with one arm while she held the boat steady with the other. "Crawl!" she said.

"Yeth," said Lou.

She was halfway in when there was a halloo from the beach. In fact, there was hallooing and hallooing.

"There she is," said The Fair Christine, looking round. "She's running."

Edie gave one swift peek. G-nan was *trying* to run, but

it is not easy to run in sand. She kept her own voice as slow and steady as she could. This was the crucial moment. She had better win. Squatting, she gave Lou's fat fanny a good firm push. Naturally she fell flat on her face on the middle seat. "Get up," said Edie, "and get in the bow." Lou scrambled. "Chris," said Edie. Oh Lord, Oh Heavenly, Oh Spikes, that was G-nan's feet on the pier. "Just move over and hold the float for one second. Hurry." Chris did it of course. The Cares all wondered sometimes how The Fair Christine was the way she was. Edie took one long step to the cleat on the float that held the dory. G-nan was almost trumpeting like an elephant, and she was on the gangway down to the float. Edie turned. Very, very carefully she stepped daintily from the float into the very middle of the dory. "Get down on the floor, quick," she said to Chris, who did it, and Edie had the stern seat free. She had picked up the jib rope and pulled it taut; then she found the mainsheet and she leaned her body against the tiller. Just as G-nan flung her mighty self flat on the float and reached out an arm, the dory leaned over and took the wind. It didn't take G-nan a second to decide to swim after them. She was a terrific swimmer and could do the Australian crawl, which even Theodore didn't know. But she didn't have on a bathing suit; she had on a long skirt with buttons and there was a lovely breeze. It was a relief to Edie. If G-nan had really caught them, she would have had to bang her fingers with an oar. After that, of course, she would be a real criminal exactly like a pirate. While G-nan was getting back to the float when she saw she could not swim fast enough, Edie put her boat in order. She located the bailer, saw that Lou was sitting properly, rescued Christine, tied the centerboard rope, and looked for her oars. She could not find any. She would not have been able to get G-nan's fingers off the side of the boat after all. Phew, what a close call! But she would have to have oars. Anyway one. She was too well trained to go without them. Halfway down the harbor was one boat she had not noticed that had not gone out. It was Shaw Wells's. He was always fussing around with his boat, but he never seemed to go out. She put over the tiller and started tacking down to him. It was too bad; it would take her a long time, but the races were always late in starting and she would have a fair wind back through the narrows and out into the bay. She had forgotten all about G-nan. She had almost forgotten about everything except herself and the boat.

"Mith-thes," whispered Lou from the bow, using her whole body to say it, "is this the ocean?"

"No," said Edie, absent-mindedly, "it's just the harbor where we go swimming."

"*I* feel like the owl and the pussy cat," said The Fair Christine. "*She's* still there," she added, looking over the water at G-nan who was standing on the float with her hands up to her face.

"There's not one thing she can do," said Edie complacently. "Everybody who can sail has gone to the races."

She did not mean to, but when they reached Shaw Wells's boat and ran alongside, she bumped it slightly. He happened to be in the cockpit bending over, so that it bumped him a little too. He stood up, annoyed.

"Oh, it's you," he said. "Don't you know how to sail a boat yet?"

He had to waste time looking at the bump.

"Would you," said Edie, "lend us a pair of oars?"

"No," said Shaw Wells.

"Would you lend us one?"

"No, did you think you knew how to sail for heaven's sake?"

There was a dent in the paint on his boat as big as a pinhead.

"Yes!" said Edie boldly.

"Since when?"

"Since a hundred years, pig," said Edie.

"You better not take those kids out of this harbor, pig yourself," said Shaw.

"I'm coming aboard," said Edie. She was bigger than he was. "You keep still," she said to Lou and Christine.

"You are not," said Shaw, and he lifted the oar she wanted and held it high but dangerously over all their heads. Edie shoved off. "I would hate to be such a dog in the manger," she said.

"I would hate to be such an owl and a puthy cat," said Lou softly. "Mith-thes, can I put just one hand in the water?"

"No," said Edie crossly. "Sit still."

"I have done it," said Lou. "I have put my hand in."

"Has she?" asked Edie.

Chris looked under the sail. She nodded. "She's painting the side of the boat with the rope," she said.

Edie let out her sail and ran sweetly up the harbor. There was a good-enough breeze, so that she had no trouble, only every once in a while Lou got tangled up in the jib and was so annoyed she tried to bite it and hit it with her fists.

"It might push her in," said Christine, watching.

"Go get her," said Edie.

They were stumbling back over the seats as they went past the float. G-nan was still there. Edie did not notice her at all. A revenge like this was almost solemn, and she was not going to make any mistakes. She ran the dory as close to shore as she dared and then set her on a straight course out the mouth of the harbor. The tide was slack and the usual tugs and pulls of the current that ran out through two pieces of land to the open sea were missing. She would have to look out for them on the way back, but now it was clear sailing round the point into the bay. Ahead of her the white butterflies were forming and dispersing, forming and dispersing, jockeying for position. She hoped she could get there in time just to say "hello" to Theodore. In the meantime, if Lou would keep still, they could all enjoy a sail, but Lou kept getting up on the seat and sliding off again in a sort of game. It became more and more frantic.

"I suppose she might be seasick," said The Fair Christine, relaxed with her hands in her lap. Presently Lou sat still, hunched up, and began having the hiccups. She put her thumb in her mouth as a sort of stopper, but the hiccups came through just the same. She looked like a fat mechanical toy whose clock work made it heave every so often, and her enormous hazel eyes kept looking all around without her head moving.

"Give her the end of the mainsheet," said Edie, "and let her paint some more."

But Lou would have nothing to do with anything but her thumb. She drew her head into her shoulders and looked up at Edie mournfully. Edie took her eyes off the sail for a second and looked at her. While she was doing it, Lou's eyelids fell down and she slipped onto the floor boards sound asleep.

Edie leaned back, pleased with absolutely everything. "I never saw such a blue day," she said.

"It's as blue as nothing," said Chris enthusiastically, squeezing her hands with her knees.

"What kind of a thing to say is that," said Edie disgusted. "Blue as nothing!"

"Well, nothing could be bluer," said Chris with certainty.

Edie felt as if she should keep on arguing to straighten Chris out somehow, but after all nothing *could* be bluer, and it was all haloed in silver and gold, the far land and the near sea. The dory was not the fleet-hulled cutter that she would have liked, slicing the waves and leaving behind a foaming, curling wake. It was a good deal like a farm horse, but it went along fast enough for the waves to slap it nicely, it held the breeze so that the sails were taut, and it was getting them there. Besides, the sun was hot; it kept you in a sort of garden of hotness while the breeze blew all around. Edie's heart was terribly thankful. She carefully did not praise herself. *That* feeling she cuddled at the bottom of her stomach like food to grow on. Perhaps already she was a couple of inches taller. She had managed things! But, of course, there was danger ahead. Theodore was a good sailor, too, very good, and he had a good boat. He might feel like boarding her and taking her and the children home and giving them to G-nan. He would do it if he thought it was a good thing to do, and she would be helpless. She kept resolutely on because she was going to chance it. She did not believe that Theodore would let anyone else sail his precious boat, especially not Jane, who he said was an idiot in boats, and especially not Hubert, who, although he looked so exactly like a sailor, could not sail at all. So it wasn't very likely that Theodore would try to pilot her back and leave his boat to *them*.

"We're almost there," said The Fair Christine suddenly.

Edie looked under the boom. They were just on the edge of the circling, tacking butterflies. She let go the mainsail and went off down wind so that she would not get anywhere near the starting flags. The breeze was a little fresher in the bay, and the dory seemed almost like a real boat. Some of the fleet noticed her and came over to take a look, but no one said anything. People did not talk much before a boat race; they just looked each other over in a suspicious way. There was no sign of Theodore. Maybe he was going to be late. Edie pulled in her sail and came about, and the dory, catching the wind, leaned over. A little spray dashed across the bow. Chris got it full in the face, and a little salt rain fell on Lou. She kicked out her arms and legs as if she had been jerked and then relaxed again; Chris only licked her face as far as she could reach.

Edie could see that the butterflies were lazily sailing in narrowing circles to be ready for the start, and she thought that perhaps after all she would go right up among them. It would certainly be a terrible thing to do to annoy all those good sailors, but how else was she to annoy Theodore? It was he who had put the enemy on her track. And he had laughed. And he had gone off racing without her when he knew, he absolutely knew, that they were the sailing people in the Cares family. She had been his crew for weeks, taking orders, getting wet, polishing brass, swabbing decks, and they had won two races together. What did he *think!* On her next tack she brought the dory so near the wind that the mainsheet crept a little, and she pointed its bow right for the middle of the jockeying boats. She had not noticed what was behind her and neither had Chris until there was a shush in her ears. Then she turned. There was Ted on the same tack as herself, easily overtaking the dory. Hubert was stretched out enjoying the sun, and Susan was lying on the weather rail, her chin on her hands, adoring Theodore. He was leaning forward under the boom to see how near they were. They came alongside very easily and took their wind, so that the dory rocked back and forth with loose sails.

"You go home," said Theodore furiously.

"Go home bad dog," said Edie freshly.

He was near enough to see into the boat, and all the talking had waked Lou. She stood up with her thumb still in her mouth and looked around bewilderedly.

"Where did you get those children?" said Theodore. "You ought to be ashamed."

"You taught me to sail," said Edie, more freshly still.

It was all they had time for. Edie heard Ted ask Jane to see if the boat hook was under the cockpit seat, so while she was feeling, Edie jibed. It took her right away from the *P.D.Q.,* but it jolted the dory a little and made Lou sit down hard on the floor boards. The Fair Christine as usual had watched what was going to happen and crouched in time.

"I want to get out of here," said Lou, getting up and climbing onto the seat.

"You sit down," said Edie, "and keep quiet. We're out sailing."

Theodore had shot yards and yards in the other direction, and Edie did not think he was coming after her. Wasn't that the starter's gun? And he was in a perfect place. She tacked up and down a few times more, but it was dull now that the fleet was off, so she thought she might as well go back. She would have to tack until she got to the point and then would have a fair wind home to the dock. Never, simply never, had anyone had such luck. Maybe she ought to ask to go to church on Sunday so that she could say a prayer. And she was glad that it was time to go home. The wind, unlike most afternoons at the beach, was dropping. It wouldn't matter a bit once they were in the harbor, but she would like to get past the commotion of the tide rip that led through the narrows out to sea before it died altogether. There were some awfully black clouds coming up in the west. The dory began to pound a little, yawing this way and that.

"Mith-thes," Lou said, standing in front of Edie with her hands behind her back, "did you hear what I said to you? I want to get out of here."

They were getting into the tide rip and Edie had no time for her.

"You'll have to walk on the ocean," she said absent-mindedly.

Lou turned and started for the bow of the boat.

"She's going to try to do it," said Chris hurriedly.

"Catch her!" said Edie, watching her sail and feeling the tiller.

But it wasn't so easy. Chris could stop her, but she could not get her back; she could just pin her down against the centerboard and Lou was kicking and shouting.

That Lou, Edie thought. She wondered if she could reach from the tiller to Lou's hind leg. Going with the fair wind, the boat almost took care of itself now that they were nearly out of the tide rip. She slipped like lightning from her place on the rail, made one turn round the cleet to hold the sheet, slid the tips of her fingers down the tiller, and reached as far as she could. Not far enough. She made one swift dip with her body, caught Lou by the back of her pinafore, and lifted her back to where she could look after her. She unwound the mainsheet rope and settled back to steady the tiller with her body. There was no touch of wood under her arm. She looked. There was no tiller. It must have broken, it must have come off; she would have to use the rudder with her hands somehow. With her left hand she felt for it. But there was nothing there. No—feel—of—wood. No rudder! She took her eyes from the sail, from Lou, from the restless water, and twisted round to look over the stern of the dory. The rudder was gone. She looked for it behind them. It was not even to be seen. Her thoughts rushed like race horses. They would not drift onto it because it had been carried she could not tell where. She must have forgotten to tie the little rope that kept it from slipping out of its sockets, or the rope had broken. With something inside her that was almost like thunder she remembered that she and Susan had been going to get a new rope and hadn't done it and that she had come out without oars. "*Never* sail without oars," was one of Father's rules. She could have easily steered home if she had had one.

Edie saw now that they were drifting fast because the tide rip had caught them. They had just not gotten out of it. It simply meant that they would go out to sea instead of being pulled into the narrows; she and Madam's two children. And it wasn't a very nice day any more either. Clouds in the west were like ink, and the wind seemed to be in gusts. There were no real waves, but there probably would be. "I have got to do something quick, I have got to do something so quick that it must be this second," she said to herself.

"Chris," she said, "we've lost the rudder. I can fix it, but you have to hold the sail. Can you? Wait till I say, then use two hands. I'll put a half hitch round the cleat."

She did it all like lightning and Chris did what she was told, steady and solemn. Edie tipped Lou over on her back like a beetle and reached into the bottom of the dory. With a jerk she picked up one of the floor boards. It was spaced, but perhaps it would do.

"I hate you, Mith-thes," said Lou. She was having a hard time getting up.

Edie drew the mainsail taut and gave Chris the end. "You have to hold it," she said. "No matter what."

"I will," said Chris.

Edie leaned over the stern with the floor board and plunged it into the water. The first time it would not stay down, so that she had to lean farther. With her hair and forehead almost in the water she clasped the wood in such a way that it took the pressure of the water at last. She felt the dory steady and begin to inch forward. She dared to raise her head and look. It was working and they *were* going ahead. It was harder to believe than anything that had ever happened to her, even anything on this remarkable day. First they were all going to be dead, and then maybe they were all going to be saved. She was not yet quite sure, but the strain on her arms was getting a little less, which must mean they were getting near the mouth of the harbor. She hung down again almost upside down using her arms like clamps, keeping the dory strained against the floor board.

"My hands hurt," said Chris.

"Her handth look like lobsterth," said Lou. She was sitting in the bilge water that had been under the floor board and was having a good time bathing.

Edie was able to get one eye up over the stern. Chris had wound the mainsheet round her hands and it was very tight. But Edie could not leave the rudder. She could not even let go with one hand. "Just one second more, Chris. Just one second." The next time she twisted up Chris's hands were blue, and great big tears were coming out of her eyes one by one. "All right, let go," said Edie. They would have to drift back a bit. This time she would put a full hitch round the cleat and be very, very careful herself not to let the boat yaw into a jibe. Chris was holding her hands in the water, and the dory was losing way. "Take it once more, just once more, and don't wind it round and round—do it just once." Edie lifted the floor board back into the water. O Lord, O Lord, they might have lost too much. They were on the edge of the tide rip and almost crossing into quiet water. They would still have to work hard, but at least they would not have to worry about going out to sea. But Lou did not know anything about this.

"She's coming," said Christine.

Edie felt a soft, solid body against her legs. "Did you hear what I've been saying to you a hundred times?"

"Go and play with the water some more," said Edie.

"I'm going to help *you,* Mith-thes."

"No!"

"Yeth!"

Lou climbed on the seat at Edie's side and put her fat hands on the top of the floor board. It wavered. "I'm sthreering," said Lou. "Chrithtine, I'm sthreering this boat." The dory came up into the wind. "Let go the sheet, Chris, quick," Edie said. She had to lift the floor board clear of the water and over Lou's head. They began drifting back again. It's like a nightmare, she thought. I wish it was a nightmare and that I'd wake up. She picked Lou up with two hands by the waist and Lou tried to give her a hug and kiss. "Later," said Edie, "I'd love to kiss you later." Rather hard and as fast as she could she put her down between her hard brown legs. "You've got to keep still, do you hear," she said. "Louli, keep still." She fastened the mainsail again and handed the rope to Chris. "Now!" Again they had drifted, but they were nearer the harbor mouth than before. She held Lou as gently as she could, but she held her tight and when she squirmed, she held her tighter.

"I would like to get out of this plath, pleeath," said Lou. "I don't like it in here. Itth too narrow."

Christine suddenly leaned over her. "Keep still," she said

right into her face. "Do you want to be dead and drownded?" She got back on the seat. "You can't swim and the fishes would eat you," she said, nodding, "all but the bones."

It impressed Lou. She put her thumb in her mouth and sat down on Edie's ankles, leaning against one of her legs. "I *don't* want to," she said, over her thumb, after thinking it over.

Going down the harbor was easy enough. The floor board made a fine rudder in quiet water, and Edie knew just how she was going to make her landing until she saw that G-nan was still on the dock. Probably she had never left it. Practically upside down with her hair dripping into the water and her arms stiff from being clamps, she realized that it was no good thinking they could go round the harbor until G-nan went away. She would never go away until she got The Fair Christine and Lou. That made up Edie's mind. To tell the truth, she was tired of them, especially that Lou. Chris was a wonder. They could never have been saved without her. But just at the moment Edie did not want to have to take care of anybody but herself. She would take the kids in, but if G-nan tried to capture her, she would use the floor board.

"Chris," she said, "the minute I start to come about let go the sheet."

She came alongside the dock beautifully, and Chris did things exactly right. They rocked gently, rubbing the old wood, with the sail fluttering in their faces. Edie left the stern and held on amidships so that the children could crawl over the side. G-nan did not move; she stayed with her arms folded in the middle of the dock. Edie wondered if she were going to wait to attack her until she thought the kids were safe. She would watch her every minute. Christine stepped onto the seat and very properly onto the dock, Lou scrambled, but both of them ran and threw themselves at G-nan's knees. "Did you thee us on the ocean?" said Lou. "*I* was sailing," said Christine, stepping back. "I had to sail because we lost our rudder."

Edie looked up for a second from where she crouched. "I brought them back perfectly safe," she said.

G-nan looked at her. "I have telephoned your Aunt Charlotte," she said, "to tell her what you have done."

Edie turned her back on her immediately. She would risk anything rather than look at her. "Well, skunks will be skunks," she said quickly.

G-nan turned and started toward the gangway. "Wait for Mith-thes," said Lou, hanging onto her skirt. "I want to wait for Mith-thes."

"So do I," said The Fair Christine. "She saved our lives, you know. She and I did together, you know."

But G-nan picked up a hand of each one of them and they had to go. Edie could see that Lou did her best and had to be carried like a monkey on a branch up the slope to the house.

Edie put up the dory, rolling up the sails and putting them away in their bag, taking out the centerboard, making the boat itself good and fast. It was frightful about the rudder. Perhaps if she went along the beach she might find that it had drifted ashore. First, however, she unstepped the mast and took it to the boathouse. As she was coming out, she remembered her fifty-cent piece and felt in her pocket. Of all the luck, it was still there! But she would not trust Fate any further. She dug a hole by the wooden upright that held up the boathouse roof, wrapped the money in a leaf, and put it in. It would not pay for a whole rudder, but she could offer it at least as a beginning. Then she went up through the ravine to the top room where she had left Widgy and wrenched open the door. "Here, Widge," she said, "here, old boy." She expected to hear a rustle in the semidarkness and have Widgy come shooting out of it to greet her, but there wasn't a sound. She went all over the room calling; she went out on the balcony to look there. He might be asleep and not have heard her. But she did not really believe that. She really believed suddenly and furiously that that gorilla had taken him, that she had done something to him. Perhaps she had killed him. Drowned him. It was what she had thought up as a punishment. Edie shot out of the boathouse, banging the door behind her, and raced down the little hill to Aunt Louise's front hall. Gander was there picking up things that had been lying around.

"Where's Miss Black," said Edie. "Have you seen her?"

"I have not then," said Gander. "Is it you are the wicked girl has the life tormented out of the poor woman?"

Edie flew through the downstairs rooms and then up the stairs. No one was there. The wind was hardly blowing the curtains, which made the rooms seem emptier than ever. She opened all the closet doors, brushing the clothes and shoes every which way, but there was not a sign of Widgy. "Chris," she called, "Lou!" at the top of her lungs, standing in the middle of the hall. Finally even louder she called:

"Here Widge, Widge, Widge." But the house seemed to be drowned in a late afternoon silence, and it just absorbed all her noise. She started running again and rattled down the back stairs and came out in the kitchen. Cook was polishing the stove.

"Have you seen my dog?" Edie asked.

"Sure, miss, I have him in the stove," Cook said.

Edie went on down cellar to Aunt Louise's old-fashioned laundry and the bath houses, which were under the piazza. There was nobody anywhere. For a few minutes she had to stop because her heart was beating so fast. If that G-nan had done anything to Widgy—!

But lucky for her she hadn't. While Edie was listening to her heart she heard him scratching and whining, and she found him in the laundry tub that had a wooden cover over it. They were so glad to see each other that it took quite a while for them to quiet down. Edie went out with him and lay under the big honeysuckle vine outside the laundry. She let Widgy sit almost on her head and held him with her two hands. She had to scramble when G-nan and the children came around the corner, and Widgy was behind her back.

Miss Black stopped. "You shall have your dog when you can behave," she said. "He is perfectly safe."

"Thanks," said Edie, getting up.

Miss Black stared at Widgy who was panting in the sun. "You are a very naughty girl," she said.

"And you are an old hunk of blubber," said Edie outrageously.

"Your aunt," said Miss Black, "will be here in a very short time now."

Aunt Charlotte did not come until Edie had had a chance to walk down the whole length of the shell road that bordered the harbor looking for the lost rudder. She felt very badly about it. Nobody would be able to use the dory until they got another, and if they had to wait until she could save the money out of her allowance, it would take several years. It wasn't likely either that anyone would lend her anything. It was her fault, it was bad seamanship, and it was because she had tried to play a trick. She had to find the rudder, and when the shell road left the harborside, she went along the beach. It could have been washed ashore if the wind and the tide were right. She was not very hopeful. The wind had died and the tide would have taken it out to sea, but she kept on, even trespassing on the beaches of the big shingled houses that ran out to the point, where they had breakwaters and walls to keep their sand from being washed away. When the sand gave out at the end of the harbor, she climbed over the enormous boulders at the point to get a view out to sea. There was not a sign of anything bobbing in the water, but through the outlet to the bay she could see that the racers were heading for home. And it was a good thing. There were a lot of black clouds coming up over the bay. She started back herself. There were not half as many thunderstorms at South Harbor as there were in Summerton, but when there was one, it was worse. Still, she would stay out till the last minute. Aunt Louise's house would not be very comfortable if G-nan were telling her woes to everyone and Edie had an idea that there would not be many people on her side. Certainly not Theodore. Hubert would go away and sit somewhere out of sight, Jane would just stand there, and the children were no good in a fight any time. What in the world she would do with Aunt Charlotte she did not know. She was not anyone you could talk to. She was not the kind of person who ever would listen. She would probably do something terrible and she would talk a long time before she did it. In the soft sand that made walking so hard Edie suddenly felt tired and for one second had a thought that made her weak. "If only Madam were home!" But she stopped thinking of it quick. She saw the boats go by her into the harbor and waved brightly. "Did you win?" she screamed.

"No," Jane screamed back. "Hurry up, it's going to rain."

"Hurry up, yourselves," yelled Edie. She really thought of not hurrying at all, of going somewhere else, of getting to the village and taking a train somewhere, but she looked at the sky. It was an awful-looking sky, the worst she had ever seen, mountains of black clouds with green and yellow in them, and it was beginning to blow in much harder gusts.

Edie got to the front door of Aunt Louise's at exactly the same time as Aunt Charlotte. She was standing with her hand on the screen door when the big black car with the chauffeur ran up behind her. She didn't have time to get out of the way before she was seen, so she put her hands behind her back and waited while John got out and opened the car door. He also helped Aunt Charlotte out because she seemed to be in a hurry. Edie waited for her scolding.

"Get in, get in," said Aunt Charlotte, looking carefully for the steps over her skirts and veils. "There's a storm coming."

It started in just that minute with a boom of thunder.

Everybody was in the hall. They had all come up from the boat by the piazza side, carrying the sails. G-nan and the children were in the background, and G-nan came through the crowd to greet Aunt Charlotte.

"Shoo—shoo," Aunt Charlotte said as Miss Black stretched out her hand.

"I've asked you to come, Mrs. Taylor—" G-nan began.

Aunt Charlotte surveyed her. "Stand back," she said, standing immovable herself. "Theodore, find me a proper chair out of drafts. There's a storm coming."

They all knew what to do then on account of Summerton. Whenever there was a thunderstorm there the relatives all met at Uncle Warren's house, because it was stone, and sat in the parlor with handkerchiefs over their eyes till it was over.

Theodore placed a large straw chair in the middle of the hall, where it was away from all windows and chimneys; Hubert gathered up glass ash trays and put them under the chair legs for insulation; Jane got a large napkin from the dining-room sideboard. Aunt Charlotte reached for it blindly after she had sat down, as her eyes were already covered by her jeweled hand. "Good gracious," she said suddenly, realizing that she had on a great deal of metal, "Miss Black take care of these!" She stripped her fingers and handed the rings to G-nan. While there was a heavy boom, rain started to splash down on the red tin roof covering the piazza. "You had better find these children places of safety, Miss Black," said Aunt Charlotte when the thunder had died away, looking out with one eye. G-nan was much amused.

"Surely, Mrs. Taylor, you're not afraid of a little thunder," she said.

"Never mind what I'm afraid of; do as you're told," said Aunt Charlotte.

Edie wondered if she had ever heard such beautiful words, and everyone looked at G-nan to see how she was going to do it. The Fair Christine and Lou were not sure what was supposed to happen, but they stared to see too. Lou could not wait.

"I want to be *here*," she said, walking up to Aunt Charlotte and putting her arms around her knees.

It completely destroyed the insulation.

"Remove this child, instantly," said Aunt Charlotte. She tried to brush Lou away with the back of her hand as if she were a piece of dust, but Lou was holding up her face with her eyes shut and clinging as hard as she could, while the booms of thunder were exploding everywhere. Chris stepped forward and peered under Aunt Charlotte's bandage. "She wants you to give her a kiss," she said in careful explanation. G-nan tugged and tried to loosen Lou's hands, but she was like an octopus.

"I said remove this child," Aunt Charlotte repeated, drawing herself back and waving her bandage hurriedly at the crowd. "Somebody take her away. She is dangerous."

It was Edie who thought of pinching Lou in the leg. "A

crab, Lou," she said, in a whisper, "a crab's got you. Persecute him."

Lou let go and walked away to examine her legs. "Take him off," she said. "Mith-thes, you get 'im off."

"I will," said Edie. She made a scoop with her hand just touching Lou's leg in back.

"Thank *you*," said Lou, and she put up her arms to give Edie one of her hugs and kisses. It made Edie let go of Widgy who was just as afraid of thunderstorms as Aunt Charlotte and had been trembling in her arms. She wanted him to learn bravery, but all Widgy wanted was to get under something, and the minute he was on the floor he dashed for Aunt Charlotte's spreading skirts.

"Merciful heavens, what now!" said Aunt Charlotte, shuffling her feet to get him out. Edie went down on her hands and knees.

"You better hurry," said Theodore as there was a sharp crack. "Dogs are full of electricity."

"I command you," said Aunt Charlotte, moving her feet faster, "to remove this animal."

There seemed to have come a lull or else the storm was over. There was no thunder for a while and the rain on the roof could hardly be heard. As soon as Edie had captured Widgy and sat down again, Aunt Charlotte rose. "We will go into the parlor," she said. "Edith, I have come to have a talk with you."

"Now for the inquisition," said Theodore under his breath, but Edie heard him. Well, she was going to stand up for her rights.

Aunt Charlotte had not taken a step when the crack came. It was not so much the noise as its sudden terrible sharpness. There was something like a pistol shot multiplied a hundred times, and it dropped a ball of fire right by the front door. This was perfectly round, and it whizzed out of the entryway into the hall. It missed Aunt Charlotte and everyone round her, but it headed straight for Edie. There was not even time to know that this was the end of Edie. Only it wasn't. The ball went under her chair while she sat with her feet tucked up holding Widgy in her lap. Her hair rose a little off her head and so did Widgy's—that was all. The ball crossed the parlor after it had gone under Edie, knocked down a lamp on the table, then jumped through a window and was gone. The glass tinkled to the floor. No one spoke or moved.

"I bet that was lightning," said The Fair Christine after a while.

They did not want to laugh. As Hubert said later, they were all almost dead, and Edie was dead and resurrected, though all she did was wipe her face on her pinafore and say, "I'm hot." The person who was really made queer by it was Aunt Charlotte. She said she was going to leave at once.

"Not *now*," said Theodore reasonably. "There might be another."

"I don't wish to stay for it," Aunt Charlotte said.

Nobody really wanted to keep her except G-nan, and Aunt Charlotte did not even listen to her, so they handed her her things politely. Hubert did her rings up in the blinder so that the lightning could not see them.

"But what about Edie," said The Fair Christine, backing before her as she went toward the door. "Is she good or bad?"

Aunt Charlotte turned slowly and considered Edie, who was still sitting in the same chair. Her hair had subsided, but she was able to get a few sparks out of Widgy by running her fingers lightly over his back.

"My dear Edith," she said, "I do not know whether you are being taken care of by God or the Devil. I shall not try to think." She paused to take her breath deep into her lungs. "But as your protector seems very powerful, I shall leave you to him until your parents come home."

CHAPTER THREE

Millard's Cove

When Edie got back from a visit to Susan Stoningham in Connecticut, she found changes at Aunt Louise's that she had never dreamed could happen. G-nan had disappeared and so had the new girl who was supposed to help Cook and Gander. Instead, there was a small round woman called Hood—just Hood—who looked like a popover, to take care of Chris and Lou. And besides her, there was Mr. Parker.

"Mr. Silas Applegate Parker," Jane told her on the way from the station. "He's fairly young and he's nice. He's only been here since yesterday, and he had a nightmare right away. We all had to get up at two o'clock and save him from being drowned in the cabin of the *P.D.Q.* He yelled bloody murder."

"How dandy!" said Edie. She hugged Widgy whom Jane had been thoughtful enough to bring with her. "But what is he here for?"

"Aunt Charlotte said that if he could just keep us all alive, it would exceed her greatest expectations."

"Phithers!" said Edie. "I bet that means me too."

"I bet it does," said Jane. "Did you have a good time?"

"Partly," said Edie.

She didn't think she would tell Jane, but she had found

visiting boring. Nothing much ever seemed to happen at other people's houses except changing your clothes and being polite, and what was the worst, there was nothing to eat from morning till night except at meals. Edie was glad to be back, very glad. She walked everywhere, even to the vegetable garden and the bridge over the railroad track, to make sure that nothing had changed. It hadn't. Nor inside either, except that it had added Mr. Parker, who might be an improvement Edie thought, as she was told he never did anything at all unless somebody asked him to, but was having a happy summer enjoying the sea air and Aunt Louise's red cushions. He was as long and thin as a string bean, and Cook was trying to "build him up." Everybody was enjoying this, they said, because there had begun to be not so much stew and more swordfish for meals.

Life at Aunt Louise's was also delightfully the same. Within half an hour of getting back Chris went out to see if there were any ripe mulberries, and later Edie herself found the little goat on the second floor eating Mr. Parker's straw hat.

Sport, Father's beagle, got ticks when he escaped from Hubert who took him to do an errand in the Ford.

"He was only chasing a cat down Main Street," said Hubert.

But the cat seemed to have known exactly what to do about him. By evening they had to put him on a newspaper and pull off hundreds of horrible bulby bloodsuckers while Chris and Lou squatted on their haunches and screeched with admiration.

Cook came in the next day and asked personally to see

Mr. Parker just at the time they were all starving for lunch. The little one, she said, had eaten it up.

"Not all of it," said Mr. Parker, taking off his glasses. "That would be impossible."

"She give the rest to the dog, your honor," said Cook. She added that she would leave at once.

"There's no train till tomorrow," said Mr. Parker with what Theodore called "remarkable resourcefulness."

Instead of chicken that day they had a picnic on the beach—of lobsters that Theodore was sent for posthaste on his bike, with the chocolate pie that Lou had not been able to reach. Lou had to be "sent to Coventry" Mr. Parker said, but she was able to watch them from her window. She had talked to them the whole time. "I can thee you, I can thee all of you. Why don't you come and get *me*? I did not eat a thingle thing. Never, no never."

She had sounded so sad away off up there that Jane asked to let her out. And what did she do? She was so full of stolen lunch that she walked right past them and into the water while they were all breaking lobster claws and sat down up to her neck. Jane had to save her from drowning.

Jane lost the bands for her teeth, which she was able to take out in the summer, and offered a dollar's reward for them. After Hubert's crawling all over the lawn until his pants were bright green, Edie found them undamaged at the edge of the shell drive. They spent the dollar together, however, on "eats" in the village, and Hubert said she was a remarkably good kind of guy.

Life could not have been more interesting. The only trouble with an interesting life was that nobody else could stand it, and Mr. Parker even from the window seat said he could observe that "chaos prevailed." There would have to be a set of rules. The best way to straighten everything out, he thought, was for them all to have jobs, so that when their father and mother came home it would not be to "pandemonium."

"Even Chris and Lou?" said Edie suspiciously.

"Certainly," said Mr. Parker, pacing up and down the wicker-chair room while he was thinking.

"I'll bet he hadn't thought of it till that second," Edie said to Hubert afterwards. Mr. Parker was ready for them just the same. Each one to his capabilities, he said. Chris could keep track of and pick up the magazines. Lou must let Sport in and out. Jane was to do the flower garden, which had been neglected, Hubert the lawn and cars, and Theodore was to take care of the boats. Edie had to feed the animals.

"It will never work," said Theodore when Mr. Parker went back to the red cushions. "I shall be the sole member of this family who does anything. Wait and see."

This speech started Jane, at any rate, off on the right track. She went out at once and weeded the sweet peas until they were a mass of naked stems, and Stanley, Aunt Louise's part-time man, came and looked at them and her, silently, with his chin in his hand. Chris loved keeping the magazines in order. It might be hard to get one to read, but Mr. Parker said he liked it a good deal better than having them "scattered from Dan to Beersheba." Lou was just as conscientious. She invited Sport in and out continually until the door slamming was more, Gander complained, than the

Saints themselves could put up with. "Where's that Hood?" she kept asking the air in the hall and dining room when she was stirring it up with her duster. Edie stuffed food into the animals willingly. If people thought the fruit from the dining-room table disappeared too quickly, she reminded them that it was by Mr. Parker's command.

It was only Hubert who fulfilled Ted's direst predictions. He came out of Mr. Parker's lecture yawning as if he wanted to lose the top of his head, and he went at once to the chintz window-seat cushions and gave a lecture of his own.

He had thought, he said, that they had come to the beach for a summer of complete relaxation. Hadn't he slaved all winter—

"Your marks show that!" said Theodore.

Was it his fault, he said, that he had had two of the pettiest-minded masters in school in both Latin and Greek? Or that the mathematics master had had a grudge against him? In a few years he would be a wage slave forever.

"Go away and let me rest," he said.

He did this by eating whenever there was anything in sight to eat and by leaving his couch only to lie in the sun on the float and crawl into the water and out again occasionally. He became even too weak to have his hair cut or pull up his socks, and some days he let his sneaker laces flop. Pretty soon he took them off altogether. He was giving his feet their freedom, he said. And night and day Ted could testify he wore the same T-shirt that had once been white. When The Fair Christine and Lou said he had promised to take them rowing, he said he had never told them such a thing in his life.

"Do you think I'm crazy?"

"Ith he crazy?" asked Lou.

"Yeth," said Hubert. "Now will you go away?" And he rolled up a piece of paper that came off some milk chocolate, put it in his mouth, and blew it out at her like a bullet.

Cook, Gander, and Hood began to "build him up" like Mr. Parker, bringing him extra things to eat.

"He will certainly attain the most prodigious proportions," said Theodore.

Edie loved every bit of it.

They had continual conferences about him either in the boathouse or on the *P.D.Q.*, where he could not hear them, and Edie found her suggestions as good as anybody's. In fact, they were acted upon. Jane thought he had gone into a decline, Theodore thought he was faking, and Edie was sure he was going out at night like Dr. Jekyll and Mr. Hyde. Ted said he would soon find out about that by putting a lasso around Hubert's feet after he had gone to sleep. "It might be a counterirritant, at that," he said.

"What's that?" asked Edie.

"Something that'll scratch him awake."

Edie thought it might, all right, but Hubert came down to breakfast the next morning as sleepy and calm as ever and Ted was late and not a bit calm. Hubert had woken up before him and tied him up with his own lasso. He was almost as big as Ted now though thinner, so what could Ted do except make remarks about people who thought they were smart. It only affected Hubert by making him reach for the banana Ted wanted. But he seemed to have strength enough to hold on to his half until the banana slipped out of its skin and there were two terrible crashes and afterwards Mr. Parker had to stop eating and reading long enough to catch and separate them. There was one thing about Mr. Parker. He might be thin and quiet, but several times they had noticed that he was awfully strong.

In spite of the first counterirritant not being a success, Edie thought she would try one of her own. Around three o'clock in the afternoon, which always seemed to be the time nobody was around, she investigated the kitchen closet. There, as she expected, was a nice fresh, crisp box of saltines on the middle shelf. It took only a few minutes to crumble these all up in Hubert's bed just far enough under the covers not to show. Even then he did not get counterirritated. He only came into Edie's room in the middle of the night, told her to get up while she was drunk with sleep, ordered her into his bed, and went to sleep soundly in hers. Edie might have slept too, but that Widgy finding a feast had to eat crackers all night and snuffle trying to get them all out. In the morning, Ted tipped them both on to the floor thinking it was Hubert.

"For heaven's sake," he said, as Edie and Widgy rolled out with what was left of the saltines, "is this a transmogrification? Get your kennel out of here."

So what with one thing and another, like dropping pennies on the trains as they went under the bridge, using the player piano, letting Jocko the monkey look in fat Mrs. Johnson's living-room window just once, besides all the usual things that you could do with sun and sand and water, it was much better than visiting.

But, naturally, just when Edie was sure she was as good

as anybody and that they would let her take part in everything, it had to stop.

What got Hubert out of his decline was nothing *they* were able to do but an enormous black yacht. She dared the narrows and came slowly and sedately into sight just off Aunt Louise's dock at lunchtime one day. She took up most of the harbor, and her engine room bells and down anchor made them all clutch their napkins and fly to the windows.

"Well, what do you know!" said Theodore.

"She may have engine trouble," said Jane. "Do you know who she belongs to?"

Nobody did, and because Gander squawked and hissed so much, they had to go back to the table.

"Probably the Queen of England calling on fat Mrs. Johnson," said Edie. "Hey, kids, don't eat *all* the dessert before it gets to me."

Chris and Lou immediately slipped out of their seats again and Jane followed them because she did not like the blancmange there was for dessert.

"They're sending in a boat," she reported, "and it's heading for our float."

"It's got a sailor in it," said Chris.

"Two thailors," said Lou. "It's whithing."

"It *is* whizzing," said Jane. "Probably they don't know that Mrs. Johnson is next door."

"Come back and sit down, Chris and Lou," said Mr. Parker.

"That sailor is coming to *our* house," said The Fair Christine very definitely as they got into their chairs. Lou nodded hard. "I want to thee a thailor," she said.

It was hardly a minute till the doorbell rang and Gander scuttled through the dining room to answer it. Lou went after her, but Gander was back before she had time to get through the door. Everyone looked up.

" 'Tis for Master Hubert," said Gander.

"Stop kidding, Gand," said Hubert, stretching so that his hands went halfway to the ceiling.

Gander marched up to his side and placed a card by his plate with a hard sharp snap of her thumb.

"Good heavens!" said Hubert, reading sideways.

"The English aristocracy to be sure," said Gander.

"Let's see!" said everybody but Mr. Parker.

"That little man in the white suit is after wanting an answer," said Gander.

"Good heavens!" said Hubert.

"Scat, scat," said Theodore and cleared the intervening heads out of his way by simply shoveling them off with his hands.

"Lord and Lady Throgmorten," he read aloud. "No, it can't be. Not Lord and Lady Throg, old chap?"

"You're not funny," said Hubert firmly. "There's a boy in my form. We always called him Throggy. He must be English!"

"But this isn't from dear old Throggy," said Theodore. "His Lordship and Ladyship want you to come aboard the good ship *Arethusa* for tea, wot, wot."

"Are you going?" said Edie. "I wouldn't."

She had enjoyed every bit of Hubert's decline, and it seemed too bad for him to get well so fast.

Hubert got up and sauntered out into the hall. They

could hear him as plain as day giving the sailor instructions, and Edie who went to the door could see him as well.

"My compliments," he said, making a slight bow, "and tell Lord and Lady Throgmorten that I accept with pleasure."

The sailor saluted with a sweep of his hand and was gone.

"Well, Master Hubert," said Gander, "you've come up in the world."

It was what they all most sincerely felt, but Hubert was nonchalant. He suddenly seemed to know all about high society. "It's tennis week in Newport and I'm going. See!" he said, which he seemed to think was explanation enough.

"Do you feel up to it?" said Mr. Parker.

"I shall do my darndest to pull myself together," said Hubert.

It was the rest of them, however, who pulled him together. By four o'clock, in Theodore's pants, Jane's T-shirt, Mr. Parker's best scarf, and a haircut by Gander, he stood on the dock.

"Ship ahoy," he called in a voice so tremendous no one knew he had it, and immediately the launch with the sailor put off to get him. Hubert on his way back to the yacht did not sit down. With his hands in his pockets he stood looking around the harbor and horizon as if he owned all he surveyed.

Edie thought he was more exciting than she had ever expected one of her brothers to be.

"*I* didn't know he had it in him," said Theodore.

He did not come back after tea. When the yacht sailed off on the afternoon high tide, he went with it after sending in a note, with a crown on the top of the paper, that he would be back in a week or more.

Jane was the next to leave Aunt Louise's, but not in any such splendor. She just got her racquet out of the chest in the hall, packed a suitcase, and went down to stay at the Tennis Club until she had won the tournament.

Theodore did not go away by himself—he was taken away by Mrs. Palmer, the flirtatious lady staying with the Chadwicks down the beach, and brought back every night. Not right to the door. Mrs. Palmer, since as Mr. Parker said, "she was robbing the cradle," did not want to come near enough to be seen doing it, and so she left him at the bridge. Ted came down the shell road loaded with golf clubs, yawned all through supper, and went very early to bed. He seemed to have given up conversation altogether, until one morning at breakfast when Edie asked him why he had to be so disagreeable these days.

"I bet it's that old Mrs. Palmer," she said.

"Oh, do you?" said Theodore. "Your brains must be growing. Do you know what you are?"

Edie knew danger signals when she heard them. She ate her last spoonful of cereal with great care.

"Chris," said Theodore, "see this knife?"

"Yes," said Chris gravely.

"Well, it's alive."

"No," said Chris, but she still listened.

"Yes, it is too," said Theodore. "You watch. I'm going to whirl it. Whoever it stops at is the biggest—"

"Donkey," said Chris, catching on. She had played this game before.

"In the world," said Theodore.

He spun the knife and, by a discreet poke administered at the end, it stopped, pointing at Edie.

Edie looked at her full mug of milk. Theodore cheated; he always, always cheated; it made her mad, hot and mad. But no, she was not going to do it. Hubert, when he heard about it, would only say for about the ninetieth time: "What do you stick your head in his traps for?" Instead, she drank up the milk, piled her plate with toast, rose with neatness and majesty, and walked out to sit on the lawn.

All of a sudden without any particular reason for it, the summer, which was being so wonderful, had collapsed. Day after day there was nobody agreeable around but Chris and Lou. And Mr. Parker maybe. At least he always said over his book, "Let me know if you want anything." But Edie could not say, "There's no fun any more." She could only sit on the lawn and think it while she dug a hole with a stick from one of the pines. It got to be quite a good hole in the end. Absent-mindedly she broke her stick in pieces and laid them across the top—a miniature elephant trap, she thought, as good as the ones in the jungle, but there were no miniature elephants around Mount Harbor unless you could count Cook, and she never went walking on account of her feet. Edie scrabbled up some grass and scattered it over the sticks. You could barely tell it now from the rest of the lawn. But she wasn't really interested in elephant traps. She was interested in getting out of here and leaving those awful people.

Jane, she knew, had once run away and tried to live in a tree. Just like a silly old hen like Jane. She was not going to do anything as foolish as *that*. But—her plan began to un-ravel like a thread—she would go over to Millard's Island to the cove there and stay for a while. For at least a night anyway. She could explore Millard's Island and she could —well, she would dearly have loved to be a pirate for a while but there weren't any any more—so she could settle down and be Robinson Crusoe instead.

It took Edie two days to make her preparations because they were elaborate. Food, a blanket, something to drink, a sweater and—last but not least—a pair of Hubert's old pants she had seen in the hall chest, and still further, scissors to cut off her hair.

She managed to get the things to eat by dodging in and out of the pantry and kitchen. Fruit and crackers were easy enough, but getting two lamb chops out of the ice chest was hard. She was only barely able to do it while Cook was on the kitchen balcony rattling the garbage pail, but she had no trouble at all grabbing a bottle of milk from the back steps before it had been taken in. She took them all directly to the boathouse, and from there on it was easy enough. She simply used the clamming pail to get them to the dock, and there she covered them with the dory's jib. Hood, wan-dering round attached to Chris and Lou, was the only one who might see them, and her responsibility as she had been overheard saying to Mr. Parker "did not extend to Miss Edith."

Hubert's pants were just where she thought, and having been there some time were just the right size by now. It was the scissors that caused her the most trouble. It was a mys-tery why scissors were always so hard to find; you might see

Hood using a pair to do the mending; Gander had some for flowers; Madam had a pair—new, bright, and sharp—but try to discover where they kept them! The best Edie could do was a pair with broken ends that were in the bottom drawer of the desk in the chintz parlor. These and the pants she took up to her room to await the last minute. That came after lunch on the second day.

"Let me know if there's anything you'd like to do," said Mr. Parker, settling down with his book.

"I will," said Edie. "Just at the moment I think I'll go out on the porch and swing."

She closed the door after her and pushed the canvas hammock back and forth a few times to make the creaking that would mean she was there, then leaving it swinging and bumping, she went up the back stairs to her room. The scissors and pants were under her pillow waiting for her. Now to finish the job and get away! There was no reason that she could see to have to have so much hair going round with you all your life. It was hot, it was heavy, it got full of salt water, it got snarls in it, it—it had so many things the matter with it she hadn't time to count. She was going to get rid of it anyhow. She went into the room her stepmother used at Aunt Louise's and stood before the long mirror, holding up her thick golden braid. She meant to cut right through it with a couple of good chops. But she soon found that what everyone said about hair was wrong. It was much harder to get rid of in her case than to grow it. No matter how frantically she brought the dull old scissors together, they just turned sideways and refused to work. She grew so angry with them they slipped out of her hand and clittered along the floor. Gander, of course, happened to be going up by the front stairs to her afternoon rest, and she looked in.

"What's the commotion?" she asked. "And in the Madam's room too. What are you after doing in here, Miss Edith?"

"Just looking at myself in this mirror for heaven's sake," said Edie, looking at herself so that Gander would go away.

"That's the ticket," said Gander, becoming interested. "Sarah Burn Hard to the life."

"I was only trying to cut my old hair ribbon," said Edie, "but there never is a pair of scissors in this house that would cut a custard."

Gander went on upstairs naturally when she heard that. All she said was not to litter up the Madam's room because she had just cleaned it. But it got her out of the way anyhow and left it clear to find a carving knife in the pantry—Father's best in the green plush case. *That* worked. The braid came away as neat as a bunch of clover. It made her feel a little scalped as she held it in her hand with the ribbon still on the end, but she shook her head and enjoyed being so light-headed. Now! It took two and a half minutes to get into Hubert's pants and an old riding shirt of her own and to tie a sweater round her waist by its sleeves, giving it a good tight jerk at the end. As she went out the door to the side veranda, she gave the canvas swing another slight push so that Mr. Parker would hear it in his dreams and feel comfortable. Not that she was doing anything she shouldn't because Father's rules allowed sailing in the bay to the end of Millard's Island and he only hoped that any child of his would keep an eye on the weather. That she was doing, though it didn't need it. It was a golden day, with great big tumbling clouds that would disappear at sunset and breeze enough to fill the sails, but which would get lighter later on. By the time she was at Millard's Cove it would blow her into the "gut" and then be as calm as soup. She might even have to row, but that was all right. She glanced comfortably at the oars nicely shipped on the dory bottom and the oarlocks hanging by their strings. This time she had not forgotten anything. The rudder for which she was still paying every week's allowance and had mortgaged what any relations might donate for Christmases or her birthdays was securely tied and the tiller tightly and comfortably held by a raised knee. She thought as she came out of the narrows into the blue of the bay that this was the right thing to have done. She expected that Mr. Parker might worry a bit, but it had made her freer not to report where she was going. She was free as a sea gull, and the whole world was glancing and glimmering.

The fair wind got her to the passageway far too soon. She could have gone on around the world without any trouble at all. Oh, how she loved boats and what you could do with them! When you were in one, it almost became yourself obeying the wind and water. No, better than yourself. It could do more and looked better. This old cow itself was doing everything exactly right. The centerboard gave a little jump and settled down again. They were over the bar. Good old cow! Wonderful old cow! As the cove opened out before her and she saw the crescent of yellow sand that ran all round it, she could not help but think that she liked it just as well—well, maybe more, than her brothers and sisters. She had been to Millard's Cove before—they all had. Now it belonged to her and nobody else—the sand, the clear water, the scrubby pine that she could smell already, the waving moor grass that covered its background hills, and the blue sea and white sky that was behind them all. Of course, not *really*. Millard's Cove and Millard's Island belonged really to the Fawkes family who liked it so well they never went anywhere else or allowed any*thing* else to come anywhere near them—no telephones, no automobiles, no electricity—not even things for grown people like cigars, cigarettes, and whiskies and sodas. Old Mr. Fawkes, who had once governed a real island for the government very kindly, governed his own island very strictly. Father had often said so. He and Madam knew old Mr. Fawkes and had been sent invitations to dinner by the food launch that came to Mount Harbor twice a week. They had to wear their best evening clothes when they accepted, though it was still the food launch that took them back and forth. Well, thought Edie, let 'em own it. They did not mind how much you used their island as long as you picked up papers and watched your picnic fire carefully. She meant to obey both rules, and they need never know that she owned the island too.

It was a long time from sunset, but it was beginning to be late afternoon when Edie was at last ready to swim and enjoy her domain, and instead found herself going distracted and wishing she was dead. She had worked the dory up the beach to safety as the tide came in and put the looped painter over a good big rock. She had got everything out of the dory and made herself a shelter in a clump of pines; she had collected rocks and driftwood to make her fire for the lamb chops and put her pail with the fruit and crackers nearby covered by her sweater to keep out the ants; now she had put on her bathing suit and meant to take time to watch a small animal of some kind that looked like a mouse nose about in the beach grass—when the mosquitoes began. She wanted to look for shells awhile, but she found herself slapping and scratching so often she gave it up and rushed into the water. There she forgot the mosquitoes on account of the wonderful excitement of the tide. There was a place you could step into the water in the cove where the tide would pick you up, whirl you through the "gut," and cast you up on the sand around the corner. She tried it over and over again, slapping absent-mindedly as she walked back to her starting point. It was when she was so waterlogged that she had to come out that she was forced to keep saying, "Golly, oh golly!" as she danced out of her bathing suit and into her clothes. It was cool enough to put on her sweater, but there was still a lot of leg and face and neck to try to keep them away from. "Smoke," she thought frantically, "smoke, smoke, smoke, smoke, they don't like smoke." She would start her supper fire and after the chops were done would put seaweed on it and make what Father called a "smudge." All the time she was getting the stones in place and breaking twigs, the mosquitoes were at her. Her paradise had turned into a place full of fiends. She covered her legs with the dory's jib as she crouched by her little starting blaze, singeing her hair as it got hotter, and when the chops were done, hardly daring to put her hand out to hold the fork to nibble from them. Before she went on to fruit and crackers she ran up and down the beach collecting seaweed as fast as she could. It made a good smudge just as it was supposed to, but it was almost as bad for her as it was for the mosquitoes, and she ate a pear drawing little sobbing breaths of fury and despair. An enormous fear began growing inside her. What was she going to do from now till morning? The tide would have turned—it wouldn't be full for hours —and she could never run the dory back against it without wind. "Golly, oh golly," she whispered through a mouthful of pear with her eyes streaming.

"Are you trying to cook yourself?" said a voice from the sky.

Edie jumped. I bet it's God, she thought wildly. He had sent the mosquitoes and now come to see how His punishment was getting along. She wasn't going to answer, although she would have to keep on slapping mosquitoes.

"What are you up to?" the deep voice said. "Come, speak up!"

"Go away," said Edie in her frenzy, "go away, go away. Can't you see I'm nearly dead already." She grabbed the back of her neck. "You can come back later and get what's left. I can tell you it won't be much." She pulled the jib up over her neck and crouched still nearer the fire, which was getting feebler. Why didn't He go! She would have to get more sticks and she knew she mustn't catch sight of Him. She had certainly heard about somebody who had tried it and been struck dead on the spot.

"I belong here," said God, "and am driving sheep."

Just what He should be doing, of course! Well, if He was

that kind of a person, why didn't He rescue her? Anyway she had better not be so fresh.

"I'm being eaten alive," she said with miserable politeness, although she thought He might have seen that by this time. "Can you get rid of them or something?"

"Perhaps I can," said the Voice. "But will you do something for me in return?"

"Yes!" said Edie. Even if she had to go to church every Sunday for a year! While tears from smoke and relief ran down her face, she thought how wrong the ministers were. You *could* bargain with God! What a mercy! as Nurse used to say.

"Hurry," she said, "please hurry. What is it?"

"I need an extra boy to ride herd," God said. "There's a gap in our line."

"I'm a *girl!*" said Edie. Maybe he wouldn't take her, but she wasn't going to pretend to be one of those animals.

"Can you ride?"

"Yes!"

She had to stand up because the smoke was practically gone, and the mosquitoes were at her everywhere. She tried to get at them by rubbing and whacking and moving while she still kept her eyes on the ground.

"Here," said the Voice, and something landed with a small puff of sand at her feet. "Anoint yourself with that."

Afterwards Edie was sure she had smelled it even on the way down from his hand. "Citronella! Golly, oh golly!" She might have known God would have some. That was what Father used on camping trips. They, themselves, took it on picnics. Why hadn't she remembered? She took as much of a bath in citronella as the small half-full bottle would let her have. "Thanks, oh thanks," she kept saying. "Thanks, thanks." She forgot, as the mosquito fury lessened, to keep her eyes lowered, and when she put up her chin to rub underneath, she looked square at the Voice. Her hand didn't even stop rubbing. There up against the sky was a tall old man in blue overalls on a cow pony. He didn't have a halo and he didn't have a beard. She got it straight in an instant, now that she could think again. It was Mr. Fawkes, of course—he looked so much like a hawk she could tell—and she had heard about the summer sheep drives. It was awful to think you could go so crazy. God wouldn't be liable to come down to Millard's Cove just for her. It was the biting that had done it. She still had to scratch a bit, but the terrible biting had stopped and she was all right now. As soon as she was anointed from head to foot, she stepped up to him and handed him the bottle.

"What do I do now?" she asked.

"Can you run at my stirrup for a short way?"

Edie thought she could. But first she would have to put things straight at her camp and douse the fire. Mr. Fawkes waited for her, and his horse stood as still as stone. He nodded approval when she was ready.

"Catch hold now," he said and turned his horse up a path through the brush that she had not noticed.

Without any explanations or reasons, just as if he were God after all, Edie found herself—in a few minutes—on a horse of her own. She had no idea why it was tied to a tree in a clearing or where the hordes of boys and girls came from who gathered there and wheeled around her as she was getting mounted. Mr. Fawkes gave her instructions. She was to ride between two boys called Bill and Charles, who at once came up to claim her, and starting at the south shore when a gun sounded, they were to beat their way back with the rest of the line to a place called The House. They were to make as much noise as they could or wished to and investigate the hills, valleys, and clumps of trees for sheep.

Mr. Fawkes might not be God, but this sounded exactly like heaven just the same, Edie thought. He tightened her girths and shortened her stirrups himself.

"Follow us," the boys said.

She was shown where to take up her station and told how to ride from side to side of the territory she was to cover.

"So long," said the boys, and went off in opposite directions to take up their own positions on either side of her.

"Not a sheep must get through the line," Mr. Fawkes had said.

If it did, she supposed, as she waited for the gun, he might have to go looking for it on a Sunday, as it said in the Bible, and then she had to remind herself that Mr. Fawkes wasn't in the Bible at all. It was still hard, she found, not to get it mixed up.

Then the gun sounded, and there was a thread of cheering that ran up and down the whole beach as the line started forward. It made a kind of quicksilver run through her heart. After this all she knew or felt was that she was on a

magic horse who did whatever a touch of the reins told
him to, that she galloped over her part of the moor back
and forth like the wind, that there seemed to be no holes or
rocks in the way, and she herself could ride better, faster,
and more skillfully than that long-leggéd boy she had always admired who rode his wingéd horse up to the sky.
Later she wondered if perhaps a sheep had got past her. She
was afraid that part of the time as she charged up and down
the little grass-covered hills she had been partly blind. The
setting sun had turned every blade of grass to fire against
the dark-blue sea, and it got a little in her eyes. Also there
was something special about breathing the kind of air that
there was on Millard's Island. It was cooler than the main-
land, and at the end of every breath was what she now
thought the most wonderful smell in the world—just a tinge
of citronella. Every once in a while she had shaken back her
lovely short hair.

At the end of the ride after the sheep had been shooed
into pens and corrals, Mr. Fawkes rode in and out among
the riders and told them to leave their horses and meet at
the bonfire. Edie, walking stiff-leggéd in the midst of the
crowd, thought she had better find her way to the cove.
She hadn't been invited to *that*.

"You're going the wrong way," said Charles's voice behind her, and he and Bill were on either side of her again,
and somehow they turned her about and made her go with
them. They were as old as Theodore, but they did not seem
to mind escorting her at all. In fact, when some friends tried
to collect them, Bill said: "We're all right here, thanks."

Edie widened her stride to keep pace with them, but she

said, overwhelmed: "You can go if you like; I'm only ten you know."

"Only ten and yet so fair," said Bill.

"Only ten and such an equestrienne!" said Charles.

She knew they were only fooling, but she stumbled over a root just the same. She looked from one to the other quickly as she recovered herself.

"Only eighteen and yet so freckled," she said to Bill. "And such a fine forelock," she said to Charles in their own voices.

It made them laugh. "Where has this ten-year-old been all our lives?" Bill asked.

"Looking for you, of course," said Edie.

She had not known it was possible to have such a good conversation with two men.

It was nearly dark as they came out of the dirt road, and what was ahead of them looked to Edie as if some jungle people were having a celebration. Along by the water were torches, flaring and flaming, and sitting in a half circle round a dark smoking pile of something were all the sheep-herding people with their heads bowed over their hands.

"What *is* it?" she said, slowing down cautiously.

It was true that Bill and Charles were wonderful and Mr. Fawkes the most wonderful of all, but she didn't really know any of them. They might be cannibals for all she knew. This *looked* like cannibals exactly.

The boys suddenly closed in on her. They each took an elbow.

"Come on!" said Bill. "I'm hungry."

"Like a wolf," said Charles.

"Tell me what it *is*," said Edie.

They simply hurried her along without paying any attention.

Maybe they were eating the poor sheep!

It wasn't cannibalism or sheep, she found, after she had waited at the place they pressed her into. It was a clambake —clams and lobsters and corn cooked on hot rocks in seaweed, and never since she was born had she tasted anything half so good. It tasted of itself and smoke, butter, seaweed, and very, very, *very* slightly of citronella. There was no more good conversation, just eating, and throwing shells into the large baskets that stood behind them here and there. That was what you did at a clambake. She was pleased that her shots were as good as anybody's.

A surprising thing happened when the clambake was almost over, and then something awful. There was a nudge at Edie's shoulder, and when she turned, she saw that Bill was being handed a guitar out of the darkness. He touched it up a little and then began to play, and Charles on the other side of her began to sing. Her heart grew so big she could hardly keep it inside her comfortably. These singing and playing boys belonged to her just like Millard's Cove. She passed sand back and forth from one hand to the other, wishing her ears were bigger so that she could hear twice as well. Then—right in the middle of a song when her head was bent—there was a silence. Charles broke off completely, and Bill let the guitar trail away in dim notes. She looked up to see another boy stepping into the circle of light waving a piece of white paper. He was breathing hard as if he had been running, but he still had lots of voice to call: "Government cutter at the southern landing looking for a young girl lost in an open dory." The circle rose to its feet. So did Bill, Charles, and Edie. "Everybody hear?" called the boy. "Anybody know anything?" There was that dreadful silence again and Edie was going to step into it when Charles and Bill moved in front of her.

"Wait!" said Charles to the air in front of him. "The Governor's going to do something."

Mr. Fawkes had risen and was walking toward the boy. He put his hand on his shoulder, spoke to him, pushed him gently out into the darkness again, and then turned to the waiting circle.

"The girl has been found," he said in his deep voice so that you could not doubt it or ask questions. "All's well. Boys, one more song—your best—and then it's 'Auld Lang Syne,' and come again next year."

"Before we do," said Charles, "three cheers for Governor Fawkes. And may we always come again next year."

The next song sounded to Edie as though it were a thousand thrushes. In the silence that followed Mr. Fawkes spoke once more. "Will Miss Edith Cares," he said, "please speak to me before she goes."

Then the circle linked arms. The boys put theirs through Edie's, and they sang together as loud as they could.

"I've got to go now," said Edie. "Thanks very much, thanks very, very much." Very politely and not at all freshly she started to shake their hands.

"Wait!" said Bill this time. "We ought to give her a souvenir. She's been our mascot all evening, hasn't she?"

"What have we got?" said Charles.

They beat their breasts and their pockets. There wasn't a chink or rustle of anything. "It doesn't matter," Edie was going to say when Bill rolled up a piece of his shirt and there was a small gold football hanging from his belt.

"My dearest possession," he said, and he hung it on a loop of Hubert's white duck pants.

"I haven't a thing," said Charles, rubbing his pockets. " 'But a poor minstrel, I!' So I think I'll give her this." And he kissed Edie on the cheek.

"You win, old man," said Bill.

"Now get!" they both said together as Edie seemed unable to move, and they turned her in the right direction and shoved her off. "Don't keep the Governor waiting."

There was no doubt at all that this was the best conversation of the evening. Edie circled the dying bonfire to Mr. Fawkes, to final capture and disgrace, hardly feeling badly at all.

Making her way by only the light of the stars down the black path she had been shown that led to Millard's Cove, with citronella in her pocket and a piece of mosquito netting folded over her arm, Edie thought about Mr. Fawkes. He wasn't God—that had been a crazy idea—but he must somehow have some connection with Him. How else could he know so much? All he had done was give her the things and say: "If you're sleeping out, you'll need these."

"But—" began Edie.

"That anxious young man at Mount Harbor," he said, "knows you are safe."

"Oh, thanks," said Edie.

"That's the path behind you," said Mr. Fawkes. "Wait for the tide in the morning."

"Oh, thanks," said Edie, "oh, thanks for *every*thing."

Her thanks were so big she didn't know how to say them. She had been almost afraid she had been going to fling herself at his feet, so she had had to turn quickly and hurry away. Now even if it hadn't been so dark, she couldn't have seen very well because of the light that kept on shining inside her. She made her feet find the way, and when the dory glimmered dimly ahead, it was another triumph.

She spent the night close to the prow in a scooped-out hollow she dug in the sand, hanging the mosquito netting from the peak o f her crossed oars, which she propped against the boat's sides. It was almost comfortable, and who cared if it got a bit wet underneath as the tide rose. On top were a million stars and on either side the noises of a sea cove—just the lap of water, the whisper of trees, and the buzz of mosquitoes outside the net. Ha, ha, thought Edie, as she was going to sleep. The smell of scrub pine and bayberry blended marvelously with citronella. She wondered half dreaming if she could now stay at Millard's Cove forever. Robinson Crusoe had had much less to get himself started with.

In the morning that sort of dream was all gone of course. In spite of the stars last night the morning was pale—she was pale and tired herself—and she thought that probably as Aunt Louise's boatman sometimes said, there was weather coming. There was enough of it here already to make quite a stiff breeze. She only stopped to eat her left-over fruit and crackers and to fold the netting carefully and put it under a rock with a corner showing so that whatever Fawkes came looking at Millard's Cove could find it. And she took a reef in the dory's mainsail. Then she had to face a problem that had been at the back of her mind all along. Was she going to be strong enough to push the boat back into the water? She hardly dared begin trying, and when she did, she realized that her suspicions had been right. She might as well try to move a skyscraper. She should have known this well enough and taken precautions. Now she would either have to stay here until she was ignominiously rescued by her family, or go and ask help from Mr. Fawkes who had trusted her to take care of herself. She couldn't do it; she simply couldn't do it. How did other people get boats into the water? She sat down on the sand biting her wrist and looking at the boat angrily. As she asked herself once more, she saw a picture of the *P.D.Q.* coming out of Aunt Louise's boathouse on rollers. If she could get the oars under the stern, the dory might slide. It worked. By putting all her weight on the very end of the prow, the boat lifted and moved just enough to settle down on the oar. Then she made some furious dashes down the beach. Luckily the slope at the water side was a little steeper and the wet sand helped. By the time it was raining hard the dory was floating and she could begin to load, and by that time too the tide was going slack. She pushed off dripping and breathless while it still had just enough strength to creep her out into the bay, and there instantly the stiff breeze caught her and she had to head straight for the middle of the rising whitecaps in order to make her next tack back toward home.

"The sail of my life," she kept saying to herself, "this is going to be the sail of my life."

She saw at once that the cove had made her miscalculate the wind entirely. It was not at all the kind of day for any dory to be out, and she wished with all her might that she weighed as much as fat Mrs. Johnson.

She made her weight do as much as it could by sitting so far out on the weather rail that she was almost in the water, but it was not enough and the dory kept shipping it in on the lee. It scared her to see the floor boards beginning to move a little; they were certainly nearly afloat. She came about as soon as she could and found it was no better on the other tack. Phithers! Although it kept her off her point and would take longer to get there, she finally loosened the jib and let it go. The dory came up. Not enough though, and it was pounding into the whitecaps and showering her with spray so that she was opening and shutting her mouth like a fish. What do I do now? she thought. I can't even see. Spill the wind, something inside her said. I've got to spill the wind. Just as things seemed so bad that the boat might go over, she let go the sheet and it righted. Between the harder gusts she pulled the sheet in again. She didn't even know it when her hands began to bleed, but she thought it took endless time to make the next tack. The dory seemed to bounce like a cork, and all the time was shipping water. This sloshed when the boat leaned and put the weight in the wrong place. She would have liked to bail but did not dare leave her place on the rail. She was just able to come about for her next tack. If she could make it for another few hundred yards, she would be in quieter water and could then shoot for the narrows, but it was the worst few hundred yards of all. Twice the gusts came so sharply and unexpectedly she was almost over, and the dory would not lift now as it had at first. It was sodden with water.

When she thought that one more gust would swamp her, the wind let up and she found herself wallowing in a kind of calm. The sudden coming to an even keel almost threw her backwards overboard. She had to pull herself back by the tiller, and she flopped onto her knees thinking the world must be coming to an end. Then she heard a purring noise behind her. She looked round and up and up and up a broad white wall. Heavens! It was the Government cutter standing off her weather quarter gently churning and purring and cutting off the wind. There was a man on the bridge with a megaphone. When he saw that she saw him, he called to her.

"Ship ahoy—stand by—we're putting off a boat to get you."

"Oh no," said Edie, but he couldn't hear. "NO!" she yelled at the top of her lungs. "NO!!" All she wanted was time to bail, and she grabbed her can that was floating above the floor boards and began to toss water over the side, letting the dory bounce.

They sent a man down from the bridge to tell her she needn't worry and to keep calm. She kept on bailing without answering. What was the use? When she heard the rattling of tackle, however, she picked up a floor board and in spite of its open spaces simply scooped water over the side.

The next time she looked, the bow of the cutter was even with the dory and the bridge was just above her. She cupped her hands. "Don't do it," she yelled as loud as she could. "I'm all right. DON'T DO IT." She had a chance to get a lot more water out as the chains rattled some more, dropping the boat. Just then she felt a little wind. She sprang back to the rail, picking up the sheet on the way and grabbing the jib as well. The cutter was falling back just enough to let the wind catch the forward sail, and the dory leaned to it at once and started going. There were all sorts of noises from the cutter, but Edie could not pay attention. She was again at sea and everything was the same as before except that the dory was alive again and would do what she wanted, and in one more minute she could make her tack and head for the narrows.

"Thanks," she yelled down the wind as she scudded under the cutter's bow. "Thanks a lot just the same."

The harbor was not a millpond as it usually was. There was still part of that stiff wind to take her, surging before it, down to Aunt Louise's dock, and Edie decided that of the whole day and night and day, maybe this was the best. She had had to have help, it was true, but only because her boat was not big enough. All that anyone could do, she had done, and here she was getting home. She wished this part could last longer. At the end of it, she had now to remember, was Mr. Silas Applegate Parker. As soon as she put up the dory, she was going to have to come face to face with him and say whatever he would think might be proper. She wished she could think what that should be.

When she got to the hall door after she had left the sails

to dry in the boathouse, she opened it softly and was going softly across and upstairs, hoping she would not meet anybody until she could change and get dry herself. If she were seen now with her hair all plastered down and her clothes plastered flat, Mr. Parker could easily think she had been drowned and her ghost was coming back—enough to scare anybody.

Her good intentions were upset by her sweater catching on the knob of the door. It made a noise and Mr. Parker was right there, his hands leaning on the window sill looking out at the bay with all his might. He whirled round and she had to notice him. At least she had to stand and look at him. He did not seem to know what to say either. He just came toward her, stealthily like a lion, with his mouth tight closed. Edie managed to speak first.

"Did you send the cutter?" she said. "It was a bright thing to do. I needed it." She nodded her gratitude. But he did not seem to hear her.

"What makes you do such terrible things?" he said.

Edie thought it over as quickly as she could.

"All you terrible men, I suppose," she said.

Mr. Parker straightened up like a jack-in-the-box and went to look out the window again. What was she supposed to do now, Edie wondered.

"Look," said Mr. Parker, coming back. "I earn my education taking care of horrible kids like you. Who do you think would ever give me another job if I let you get into trouble? Eh? Do you understand that much? Do you?"

Edie was making a large pond on Aunt Louise's chintz

room carpet, but she felt she would have to stay and get finished with it. After all he had sent the cutter.

"I don't see what you want an old education for," she said. "But why don't you keep me out of trouble then with those horrible boys?" Her voice rose. "How would *you* like being called names from day until night? How would *you* like being left alone all your life? How would *you* like to be teased till you were nearly dead? Yah!" she said, hoping she was not going to cry because she hadn't slept very well. "What do *you* understand I'd like to know?" She turned away from him quickly, and quickly made for the stairs. She was hating herself for trying to explain to that old Silas Applegate Parker. She had her own friends now, and she didn't need to ask him for help. Or didn't she? Her feet began to drag. Oh dear, she would have to go back. She went to the sitting-room door and stood with her hands behind her. Mr. Parker was sitting in a chair with his face in his hands staring at the floor.

"If you sent the cutter," said Edie loudly and firmly, "it was a dandy thing to do. I needed it badly."

The silence baffled her.

"What shall I say now?" she asked.

"It's not saying, it's feeling," said Mr. Parker.

"I feel wonderful," said Edie. "I had the most marvelous time in my life."

"All right," said Mr. Parker. He linked his hands and stretched them out in front of him as if to keep something off. "All right, all right, all *right*. No more said." He got up and stood looking down at her as she wiped back her hair with her palms. He even smiled.

"I guess," he said, "you and I better go to the barber's this afternoon. How about it?"

"All right, yourself," said Edie. "I didn't really do a very good job, but whoever can find a pair of scissors?"

As she went upstairs, she put her hand on the little gold football and thought, "It's still there. I'm so glad. It's still there." She meant to keep it forever and ever and ever.

CHAPTER FOUR

The Weather

The weather that blew up after the sheep drive at Millard's Island was reluctant to leave Mount Harbor for a single day that August. Some clear days did manage to sneak in and stay for a little while, but presently the moon had a golden ring again and the next morning it was blowing and raining like mad; mold collected on shoes; sheets were damp and cool; and Aunt Louise's began to smell of Widgy in every room.

"If this keeps up, we'll have moss behind our own ears," was Theodore's opinion on the fourteenth day of downpour.

When it rained at the beach, it made almost no difference in having a good life except to him. He could not sail on account of the high wind, and he could not play golf with the flirtatious Mrs. Palmer even if it were only drizzling.

"It might wash her off," said Hubert, but he did not say it in front of Theodore.

Hubert was back from his cruise on the *Arethusa*. The weather had been so bad that the Throgs, themselves, who were supposed to be sailors, had not been able to stand it and had brought him back in a black limousine almost as big as the big black yacht. No one had seen his arrival; but

Edie, who was on the way up from clamming, found him pushing a girl at top speed down the shell drive in a wheelbarrow. It turned out to be Lady Alicia Throgmorten, and it was obvious, after Edie had got Jane and Theodore to see the sight, that Hubert's decline was over for good. Just the same after the limousine had driven off without him, he was perfectly content to take up his position again on the chintz window seat with his feet in the air.

"Well, that's the end of that romance," said Theodore in his hearing.

"Oh dear no," said Hubert. "I've been invited out for another week as soon as the weather clears."

Mr. Parker took up the study of economics on the window seat in the opposite room, and Jane and Edie took up a daytime residence in the boathouse in order to use the player piano. By them, rain at this time was almost welcomed. The player piano, they had discovered long ago, had one hundred and thirteen rolls, and during the rainy season, they said, they meant to play them all. This was not getting done. They had got stuck at "Maryland, My Maryland" and "Marching Through Georgia," because, if they played these two tunes and one or two others just as they wanted, they could make themselves laugh, cry, be in a fury, gallop like taking the good news to Aix—anything. Edie often did not see the use of taking all the trouble people went to to learn to play the real piano when the player piano would do it just as well and do all the work besides. She was, herself, quite an expert. Perhaps you had to learn that much. But after the simple technique of pedals, speed, and stops had been mastered, *you could go!* Rollicking, dashing, headlong crashing, creeping, crawling, and softly, softly crying if you really wanted. It was the one time that nobody in the Cares family said anything about crying. You could sit at the player piano and drip tears. They were not remarked upon; all the others did the same when it was their turn. There was only one thing the matter—Widgy, on account of howling, had to spend a lot of time in Aunt Louise's cellar.

Chris and Lou, when they could not go out, played in the cupola, or on the cupola stairs, which during the rain no one dared to go and take a look at. They were conscious that Hood was allowing messes of every description, which were being stirred, dumped, spilled, and scattered—at least if the way Chris and Lou looked was any indication—in every direction, and especially on the stairs.

So when it rained unusually hard for another two days and the wind was still stronger, no one really minded but Ted. He tramped the hall and the sitting rooms after breakfast and went upstairs and downstairs looking out every window in turn.

"For the love of lollapaloosa," said Hubert, "can't you keep still?"

To him the house seemed in a particularly elegant state. On one of the good days before this last storm Lou had run her face into the corner of the small blue boat she and Chris were allowed to use when it was tied to the shore in shallow water. It had made a hole in her chin through which she could make a drop of milk and blood come out, and everyone, including Lou herself, had been delighted with it. But Hood had made Mr. Parker telephone Aunt Charlotte, and

Aunt Charlotte, because the beach was "a wilderness" that no good doctor would be likely to inhabit, had commanded Mr. Parker to drive Hood and the children up to Charlottesville, where she herself could get Lou properly plugged up. In the meantime, Aunt Louise's, with Jane and Edie drenching themselves with sentiment in the boathouse, was Hubert's ideal of how a house should be. He thought Theodore ought to appreciate it, and besides, having him walking all over the house without cessation took his own mind off Sherlock Holmes.

Just the same Ted kept on with his inside cruising and running his hands through his hair, and every time the wind gave the house a buffet he would stop to listen. He put in a few minutes at Hubert's window seat sometimes, taking the other end, and putting up his feet in the same way. He looked as if he were reading a magazine. But it apparently did not suit him, so he got up again and walked some more, jingling something in his pocket. When Hubert looked at him disgustedly over his book and Ted noticed it, he took the chance to speak to him.

"It's blowing," he said.

"Tell me another," said Hubert.

"I think I'm going out to the *P.D.Q.* and put out another anchor."

"Just as your lordship pleases," said Hubert.

"You won't come?"

"Certainly not."

Theodore couldn't make up his mind though. He took another tour, going to the top of the house and then down cellar. He looked out the dining-room window for a long time. After a particularly hard buffet he at last put on his yellow slicker, took off his sneakers, and went out the veranda door toward the boathouse. If that lump of inertia wouldn't help him, he would have to try elsewhere. Bracing himself against the wind, he knew that it was going to be a hard job, just as he had suspected, and he would need some extra hands. But Jane was playing "Old Black Joe" and "The Bells of Shandon" alternately and she did not want to go either.

"Take Edie," she said indifferently.

"Do you hear *that*," said Theodore when the wind gave the boathouse a blow.

"No," said Jane. She drew out the chorus agonizingly in order to break her heart, and hopefully Ted's too, but he had a heart of stone. She had known this many, many years.

"Come on, Edie," said Theodore. "You don't want her to go ashore, do you?"

"You never let me sail her," said Edie consideringly from the floor. She had found a nest of mice in the boathouse cupboard and had them in the lap of her dress.

Theodore would have liked to tell them what he thought of them, but he saw it was not the time for that. He would do it after he had saved the *P.D.Q.*

"Well, I will next week," he said. "If there's anything left to sail," he added, trying to make an impression. As neither of them moved, his temper rose and leaped out like a knife. "You batter-headed bone domes," he said, "are you blind and deaf? Wake up!"

Jane shut the sliding door of the player piano and covered the keys in a leisurely way.

"I don't see what you're fussing about," she said as she put on her slicker, and as she opened and shut the boathouse door easily and softly, she added: "There's no wind here."

But as they came round the corner, it hit them so hard they were knocked against the wall.

"See what I mean?" said Theodore.

"Gee," said Jane when she could get her breath.

There did seem to be a sort of gale. It licked her hair across her face, and she could see when they reached the shore the boats in the harbor bobbing and turning as if they were being whipped. She and Theodore had to shout at each other, it was true, but since the tender was pulled up on the dock, it would be easy to get her away.

After they had left, Edie put the mice back in the cupboard and opened up the piano to have her turn. She played "My Old Kentucky Home" and started "Comin' Through the Rye" but stopped in the middle because it didn't seem any fun any more. She wished she had gone with Ted. It might have been fun trying to get out to the *P.D.Q.* in the wind and rain. She just hadn't realized what was going on. With envy she watched them putting out from the dock. Crickey, the wind had whirled the tender and smashed it up against the dock cushions, and Ted was having an awful time trying to push off. She looked down at the shore and saw that the tide, which should not be high until two o'clock, was already halfway up the sand. It would begin to fill the little ravine between the boathouse and Aunt Louise's lawn pretty soon. It must be one of those big tides they talked about, and she wondered why she had heard they came in the fall. This was only August. She wandered

back to the piano after she had waited to see Theodore and
Jane finally, after a tough row, the wind pushing them this
way and that, board the *P.D.Q.* She played "Silver Threads
Among the Gold" as sadly as she could. And then "The
Rosary" and "The Lost Chord" twice apiece. She began to
be aware that no matter what she did with the stops and
pedals, the music did not quite drown out what was happening outside and it made her uneasy. She took several
looks at the tide. It was coming on like anything, and just
as she had her nose pressed to the balcony window, the boathouse started and then trembled as if it had been a frightened horse. Out in the harbor, she noticed, the little two-for-
a-cent dory of the Howlands' had turned over and was
floating bottom up toward shore. Well, it had always been
unseaworthy. She did not much care. She could also see
that Jane and Ted were managing to get out the second
anchor and felt proud of them. She *wished* she had gone.
She went back and finished the last piece, pulling out all
the stops and keeping her foot on the loud pedal so that the
music would wail disconsolately. It seemed a fitting accom-
paniment to the wind. But the wind was the strongest; she
could feel it as well as hear it, and she heard it whack the
roof so that it began to dance and flop. Just as she reached
the end, there was a wild screeching tear, two or three
mighty bangs, and the roof settled down like a wounded
animal half on and half off the boathouse. Edie covered the
player piano in less than a second, grabbed the billiard table
cover, tore it off, and flung that on too. "I guess I better get
out of here," she said to the noises all around her. But she
had to rescue the mice. Before she could get to the cup-

board, the roof gave another scream and tear and she saw it go up in the air and heard it crash away against the pine trees that bordered the drive. "Oh, the poor player piano!" Every bit of covering was ripped off it the minute the roof was gone; the billiard cover went straight up in the air, and her slicker hopped after it from the nail on the door. "Oh, the poor mice!" What could she do for them? She ran around in a crazy kind of hurry. When there was a tiny lull, she had time to pick up a mat and make a tent over the nest in the cupboard while the rain poured down her face and neck and the wind made grabs at her. Then she scooted for the door. She stepped out into a flood and saw that the tide had risen so fast and far that the ravine was full and she would have to swim for it. Not that she minded. The hard part would be getting across the lawn to the house. There the wind would catch her, and besides there seemed to be a lot of things flying through the air. One was a sofa cushion that rolled across the top of the water. Where had *that* come from? It wasn't Aunt Louise's. She wasn't quite sure that her eyes were seeing right, but she decided it must be a real gale and perhaps it came from Mrs. Johnson's.

Edie reached the edge of the lawn and then crawled along as far as she could under the lee of the blue- and bayberry bushes. The rest of the way she waded up to her knees, trying not to get knocked down by the wind. She was almost to the door when the top of one of the pine trees was swirled over her head. "That was a bit lucky," she thought, as Hubert held the door open a crack to let her slip through.

"Quite a blow!" said Hubert. "Where's Ted?"

"The roof blew off the boathouse and I had to swim the ravine," said Edie.

"I saw it," said Hubert. "*Where's* Theodore?"

"He and Jane went to rescue the *P.D.Q.*"

"Of all the darn fools. The wharf's gone, the pier's twisted into a U, and the cupola's blown off."

"How simply marvelous!" said Edie. "They'll have to swim for it. I wish I was there."

"Don't be so darn sure," said Hubert. First he looked out the window and then he turned back into the room, walked around the table, and looked out the window again.

"Where are Father's glasses, do you know?"

Edie did know and went directly to the cupboard and got them. Hubert screwed them to fit his eyes.

"It's easy enough to see that they don't know what to do," he said, and handed them to Edie.

After seeing nothing but branches and sky for a while she finally got them focused to where a tiny boat and two tiny figures could be seen, getting the full strength of the blast.

"The *Q* is going under in just about a minute," said Hubert.

Edie could see that she was well settled in the water and that Jane and Theodore were sitting precariously on the edge of the cockpit rail evidently trying to make up their minds about something. She hung on to the glasses when Hubert wanted to take them. "No, wait, wait, one sec, one sec." The funny thing about the harbor was that there wasn't a wave on it. The wind had flattened it out like a board. Still, not being able to head to the wind fast enough, the *Q* shipped some more water just before Hubert took the glasses away.

"She's down," he said after a minute with a kind of solemnity.

Edie could not see what there was to be worried about. With the water so smooth and the wind blowing toward shore, all Jane and Theodore had to do was tread water and wait. They might end up in the village instead of Aunt Louise's, but they would certainly end up. She herself would have liked to see if she could have *walked* on the water like Jesus Christ—it looked so firm and easy to do. It probably wasn't, though, because the two black specks that were Jane and Theodore's heads were bobbing along up to their necks. She followed their progress, wishing she were one of them, but she did not want to seem hardhearted if Hubert thought Ted and Jane were liable to be drowned before their eyes, so she said nothing.

Hubert put the glasses down on the table. "They're under the lee," he said. "We'll just have to wait." Something made him look down at his feet. "Holy Christmas! What's this!"

Their feet were splashing in water that Edie had not noticed because she was so wet already, and they became conscious that there was water everywhere; the beach below the house had become part of the harbor, the lawn was a salt lake, and the drive at the right, which dipped through a mound at the back of the house, was filling up with water that ran down from the lawn. It was not rushing water; it came in little waves that kept getting deeper. They had the same feeling at the same time and turned toward the hall. There was water there too, and in the dining room where they looked next, and coming downstairs, to their astonishment, there was a little brook.

"That's from the cupola," said Hubert. "And it's mixed with Chris's black paint."

"What I would like to know," said Edie, "is whether all this"—she kicked a foot—"is coming from outside or down cellar."

Funnily enough there was no water in the kitchen yet. It must have been afraid of Cook, Edie thought, like everybody else, forgetting the steps up to the kitchen. But when they opened the cellar door, they were horrified. The whole cellar was full, and on top floated a ghastly murky mess of the dirt of ages mixed up with Cook's cotton uniforms and Gander's dish towels.

But what was the worst of all, there was Widgy soaked and shivering on the top step. "Oh," said Edie, "oh, my dear little dog! I forgot you. I'm so sorry I forgot you." She grabbed him up and wrapped him in her dress while Hubert closed the door hurriedly. Then they sloshed back to the hall.

"Do you hear that?" said Hubert, listening.

The wind had taken to a high singing and was not so much blowing in gusts now as pushing with a steady terrible pressure that could almost be felt through the walls. But yes, there were gusts too that whanged things against the house or sent them hurtling past the windows before it could be seen what they were. It rattled the windows and each time seemed to fly off screeching afterwards. It was a sound that, if you were a dog, would make your hair stand up, which was what reminded Edie that no matter what was happening she would have to rub Widgy and leave him in a safe place.

As soon as she had used up her own bath towel and Jane's and commanded Widgy to stay in his bed and shut the door of her room so that he would do it, she came down again.

"Look who's coming," said Hubert, noticing her as she came up to him in the hall, his voice suddenly cheerful, and sure enough, there were Jane and Theodore sailing into the filled-up ravine as smoothly as if they were boats. What's more, as if they were being chased, a boat was coming after them, a big, elegant, white sloop—crickets! Shaw Wells's sloop had broken her mooring and was simply scudding before the wind. Theodore and Jane steered themselves neatly toward the house, swam a little way, and got to their feet in water up to their knees. The sloop just nicked the corner of the boathouse with her stern, turned in their direction, and looked as if she might still catch them before they got to the house, but she drew more water than they did, and when she met the lawn, she heeled over and had to slow down. Hubert again had the door open a crack, Theodore and Jane slid through, and everybody leaned against it to get it shut again.

"Quite a blow," said Theodore without noticing the flood and went to look out the window for the *P.D.Q.* The twenty-one footer was still there, but by this time she had settled deep in the water. It looked as if the anchors were still holding, however. It was the best he could hope for her. If she went ashore, she would be banged to bits on the rocks at the back of the sandy beaches.

"She may make it," said Hubert.

"With luck," said Theodore, "with the sky's own luck."

They could see that the harbor was being swept clean, and it wasn't taking long either. The boats looked as if they had gotten wills of their own, broken their bonds, and were all off willingly to other lives. Once free, they raced before the wind, especially the big ones. Shaw Wells was lucky. All four of them gazed and gazed, forgetting their feet and all the wet, and not even realizing that they could see more plainly from the parlor window than ever before, because one of the pines had gone, until there was a second crash and splintering and the top of another one flew over the lawn.

"Maybe we better move a bit," said Theodore. They had to walk now like ducks, lifting their feet.

"It just occurs to me that perhaps we ought to try to get some of this furniture upstairs. This tide is pretty strong."

Each one started toward what they thought they could carry, but they were too late. Ted had just spoken when the tide itself decided to take care of the furniture. They had been looking at too many other things to pay attention to the little waves that had become surges, slow, but big and very strong. There was a bash at the French door that opened toward the sea. It did not quite give, but they could hear the wave swirling off at the house corners.

"I don't believe we're going to wait," said Theodore. "Get going, kids!"

"Where?" said Jane.

"The stairs!"

They reached them just as the next bash came, and they turned on the landing. The sea curled into Aunt Louise's by way of the French doors, which it had opened, slithered through the chintz room and the hall, and swashed against the door that led out to the drive. They watched it withdraw for a minute and then come again with greater power, feeling around the legs of the chairs and trying to pull out the carpets and open the other doors. There was no letup to the wind, and there seemed to be no end to the tide. It was long past time for it to turn. They knew, because they usually went swimming at high tide and kept track of it. It was just as if the whole ocean, moon pull or no moon pull, had decided to come ashore and eat up the land.

When the next surge opened the hall door and the waters met, the ocean rushed boiling into the wicker chair room and the wicker chairs followed it out as if they had been called by the Pied Piper. They had to watch them go. But Theodore and Hubert were not quite able to bear it. They thought they could do *some*thing. They both stepped out into the hall as the flood receded, and they both were hit by the returning wave. It took their legs out from under them, and Jane had to step down and rescue them from being hit on the head by the floating sofa. She gave it a shove so that it swirled away.

"Phew," said Theodore, when they were back on the landing again. "No more of that."

"Not for me at any rate," said Hubert rather sheepishly. From then on they just had to watch the water take everything away. As it tugged away the tables, the lamps and ornaments splashed into it onto the floor, but it came back for them later. They could hardly believe their eyes at the neat way the water managed to get everything out. The sofas hardly nicked their wood.

"Well, that's that," said Theodore when the hall and the two sitting rooms were empty and the dining-room furniture was knocking and grinding itself to pieces. "I hope it leaves the house standing."

They all began to hope so, as they had time now to notice that Aunt Louise's was being hit over and over again by the wind and sea. Thoughtfully they crowded up a few steps above the landing. The water had swept up to just below them and was being added to by the brook they had forgotten that was still running neatly down the stairs.

"By the way," said Theodore, "does anybody know where those two women are?"

There was a general shaking of heads. It was the first time anyone had thought of Cook and Gander for what seemed ages.

"I have an idea we better find them."

They left the landing reluctantly, all except Edie who raced upstairs to be the first to get down the back way to the kitchen. On the way she stopped to take one look out of the upstairs hall window and make a report. "You know the bridge to the island?" she said, running ahead of them again. "That's not there any more and the Burtons' yawl is right on top of the causeway, but *that's* under water and it'll probably fall over the other side."

"You keep away from the windows," said Theodore.

"That's right," said Hubert. "Do you want to be sliced in two?"

But Edie was halfway down the back stairs. "It's coming into the kitchen now," she said, "and Cook and Gander are yowling."

"Now, Miss Edith," Gander's voice said loudly but calmly. But still they could hear her using it for something else.

"Come up here," said Theodore, starting down.

"Get on with you now, get on, I say," said Gander's voice from below.

There was a noise they could not understand that followed. "Did you hear the young man, you loon?" said Gander. "Holy Mary, get down from there and get goin'."

Theodore bellowed once more, and Gander's face shone up as white as a sheet from the bottom of the stairs, where the water was sloshing. "Master Theodore," she said. "I can't move the old basheen. She's lost her wits. Can I leave her to be drownded, sir?"

"Not yet," said Theodore. "Come on, Hubert."

The boys stepped out into the kitchen, and Jane and Edie came down far enough to see Cook sitting on the kitchen table with her eyes closed, saying her rosary. The water was curling gently here and there, but it was not very deep.

"Get up," shouted Theodore.

"I'll not move," said Cook. "Holy Mary, Mother of God. Hail Mary, full of grace."

"You'll drown pretty soon," said Theodore.

"Do I know it," said Cook, without opening her eyes. "Leave me say me prayers in peace."

"The old abadan," said Gander. "Sure, give her a pinch, your honor."

" 'Tis better than having the roof on me head," said Cook.

Theodore could feel the water creeping up on his ankles. It must somehow be coming in from the front part of the house now, and who could tell how high it would go, but how—just how—could you lift a mountain like Cook? While he was thinking, Hubert came and stood beside him, gave him a look, and made a heaving motion with his hands. Theodore understood him.

"Are you ready?" said Hubert softly, but Ted could hear him. "One, two, *three!*"

"Heave ho, and a bottle of rum," shrieked Gander. "There's the laddies."

As they tipped the table, Cook slid gently but decidedly toward the water. When her feet touched it, they began automatically to move, and Gander piloted her toward the stairs. "I've got her now, your honor," she said. "We'll sit in the middle here, and should the house come down, we'll take the bash of it and die quick."

Theodore and Hubert sped past them back to the upstairs hall. What for the love of heaven had happened to their other females? Jane and Edie had disappeared. "Well of all the—" Theodore said, but was unable to find words for them. He gave them up as a bad job. The wind was still pounding the windows and smashing at the roof, but he couldn't keep them from being fools if that's the way they were made. Still, he would have to make one more try. He stood at the top of the stairs and opened his mouth as wide as it would go. "Everybody," he roared. "Come here!"

"What's the matter with you?" said Jane just above him.

"Come here," said Theodore, "sit down right here, and stay down, darn you." As soon as he could stop roaring, he sent Hubert to shut all the room doors and stood with his head cocked. The wind was now one thin, continuing scream, and the house seemed to be leaning to it. Hubert, who was on the second floor by now, called to him, and as he went down, Jane and Edie followed.

"Take a look," said Hubert who was on the landing.

The sloop, which had come up on the lawn, had moved closer and closer so that its bowsprit was almost in the front door.

"If it comes in," said Edie, "I'm going to get aboard."

"Will you *shut up,*" said Theodore.

"You're enough to tempt God to do *any*thing," said Jane, who did not like the sound of the wind or the feeling of the house any more than he did.

It was impossible to answer because just then there was so loud a crash that nothing else could be heard. No one moved and no one spoke, but it made them all crouch as if they were going to be hit by something. Jane waited for the house to fall down, and Edie waited for something more exciting to happen, Theodore waited trying to think, and Hubert got up slowly and went upstairs to see if he could find out what had happened.

"The float," he said, when he came down and crouched on the stairs again. "It looks as if it had tried to get in the dining-room windows. I don't think it did, though, because there's no extra wind in here. It's quite a sight, though."

Jane and Edie were getting up to go and look at it when Theodore clamped a hand on each of them and kept them there for what seemed hours, huddled and silent. Finally he said slowly: "I bet, but *that* is quite a sight, too, at least for me." He pointed to a slimy, dingy mark on the glass of the flung-back French doors and gave a sort of groan of relief. The water was below it.

"The tide's turned," said Hubert slowly.

They all stood looking at it as if it could not really be there and they must keep on looking to make it true.

"Of course I knew it would," said Theodore, "but it took long enough. I'm going to change my clothes. You kids keep away from the windows just the same; the wind's still going strong."

Everyone went to change his clothes, paying no attention to Ted at all. The wind *was* still going strong, but the scream was going out of it and the house now felt again as though it could stand anything. Pretty soon, they felt, it might just be a high wind, and when the water went down, they were not going to miss the chance to explore everything that had happened. It was long past lunchtime, but no one had thought about that and they weren't going to now. There wasn't much hope that Cook and Gander would feel well enough to produce anything, so they let it go in favor of seeing what was left of the world.

When they came downstairs dry and shiny, they found Aunt Louise's lower floor becoming just like the bottom of an empty aquarium. There was green slime floating in it, shells and sand and old seaweed at the bottom of it, and after the water had gone down still more, Edie saw a crab trying to get over the tread of the veranda door. With the tide and the wind both dying, it was not very long before they could slide along the slippery floors.

"What a sight for sore eyes!" said Theodore sarcastically as they stood in front of the chintz room fireplace. The soot had been washed out and all over the walls. Hubert's favorite lounging place squelched with salt water and its cushions were probably by this time half across the bay. There was not a stick or a stone or any sign of any piece of furniture or bric-a-brac in either sitting room, and in the dining room it was huddled like a herd of sheep by the pantry door. The float had indeed been trying to get in the dining-room windows and was now sitting jauntily half on and half off the piazza rails. After taking a good look at everything, Hubert summed up the general feeling. As it would certainly, he said, take a couple of years to clean this up, they might as well go out and look around. The sky was clearing. They were all sure that before long the sun would be out bright and gleaming, and before they were caught by the two ladies "so nobly saved" he said "to continue in our service," they had better get out of sight.

"A suggestion for which you should be knighted, old chap, wot, wot," said Theodore, remembering Lord and Lady Throg.

So that just as Gander came through the door pushing a mop ahead of her, they disappeared behind Shaw Wells's sloop.

They went first to the boathouse—a sorry, sorry, journey and not exciting in any way.

"That's the last of the old piano," said Theodore, looking in the top and finding it full of water.

"Oh no!" said Edie. "Can't you fix it? Can't you dump the water out? Can't you think of a way to dry it? Can't we do it now?"

The rolls from top to bottom of the pile were drenched and turning soft. Edie wanted to take them out and hang them on the bushes. "Look, guys, the wind's gone down now, the sun's blazing. Let's do it." Nobody would. They were too anxious to see what had happened on the beach.

The mice were dead too—pinkly, wetly dead. Hubert was for dropping them into the bushes. "No," said Edie, "maybe they'll come to life like some people do." She spread them out in a row in the sun.

"When they begin to stink," said Hubert comfortingly, "don't ask me to bury them."

They were taking a last sad look at everything after examining the billiard table cover and the dripping flags when they heard calls from the house.

"They're after sending a boat from across the way," called Gander. "Your aunt's sticks of furniture's beyond on the shore. Could you get over now before the next tide and pull it back with you behind your boat?"

They thought this a delightful suggestion. The Edmunds lived almost exactly across the harbor. The tide in trying to take the furniture out to sea had been stopped by their sandbar evidently. They all started for the pier with one accord and stopped with one accord at the top of the little bluff. The float, they remembered, was sitting comfortably on the piazza, and the pier, they could see from there, had not only been turned to a semicircle as Hubert had reported but tipped over. Jane spied the skiff. It was upside down on top of the blueberry bushes that bordered the lawn.

"The oars are probably in Spain by this time," said Theodore.

Anyway they couldn't be found. Hubert found one of somebody else's—a high brown color—wedged between two rocks under the bluff, and Theodore thought he could scull across with that. What he really wanted to do was rescue the *Q,* but for that he would have to wait for the harbormaster, Captain Harbuck, and *he* would be too busy now to help with small boats.

"We can't all go, that's a cert," said Hubert after they had all helped to get the skiff back into the water. He himself stepped in and sat down on the middle plank. "I strongly advise you girls to amuse yourselves in some other manner," he said. Ted shoved off, as if he were the other brain with but a single thought, and Jane and Edie were left noisily but helplessly behind. When they saw that their case was hopeless, they started down the sand. There was no end to the wonders. The Barrons' launch was on the Lampsons' piazza, the Lampsons' own boat was missing, and *their* float was tangled up in a tree. Some parts of the shore looked like jackstraws—big wood, little wood, new, old, sticks, logs. There were smashed boats on some of the boulders and smashed windows and roofs on the summer cottages behind them. The ocean had cleaned out all the back yards and pitched up what it got just where it liked. Jane and Edie found one of the skiff oars and Jane put it over her shoulder.

"Suppose it isn't?" said Edie.

"See that peck on the leather," said Jane. "Lou bit it out because I wouldn't let her row. I saw her do it."

Every kind of work had stopped in Mount Harbor, they could see when they got to the village. The people were all on the street looking and talking. To Jane and Edie they said "Quite a blow!" They answered, "You bet!" Olsen's boathouse was right where it ought to have been, but when they looked through the door, there was nothing in it, not even a can of paint. "Lost it all," said Mr. Olsen who was standing nearby. "Quite a blow!" Opposite the station the electric light poles had lain down in a tangled, crazy row. Jane and Edie stood on the station platform and stared.

"You keep away from them wires," said Mr. Olsen, coming up beside them. "I've seen people scorched up horrid because they was ignorant."

"We *know*," said Jane.

It was terribly lucky, they both thought, that Mount Harbor had no trees or they would have all gone down like the poles. "Perhaps," Jane said, "they all went in another storm." And they had never been able to see them. She didn't know how Edie felt but she was proud of the small gray houses in the village that had sat steadfast against the storm. Their owners were airing them out now and probably trying to get the floors dry. Not one house in the village of Mount Harbor had moved an inch, nor their roofs either, nor their garden fences—or only just one at the end of the street—that was Mr. Lumsden's new ice-cream parlor. It was standing on its head.

"Oh my!" said Edie.

They were not the first ones to get there by any means; a

large party of village children were taking turns looking in the window, which, miraculously, had not been broken. Jane and Edie elbowed themselves in when they thought it was their turn, and the rapturous sight that met their eyes was one they could hardly tear themselves away from. The entire contents of Mr. Lumsden's ice-cream parlor had been upset with the house and lay mixed in "more than oriental splendor" on the ceiling.

"No, it's the floor now," said Edie, leaving the sight slowly and reluctantly. "Did you see the chocolate creams?"

"*I* looked at the gum drops," said Jane. "They look like the hard kind that last for hours."

It was like Aladdin's cave. They had not had anything to eat since eight o'clock, and all Mr. Lumsden's great glass jars had lost their stoppers and poured out bull's-eyes, rock candy, peppermint sticks, licorice drops, peach blossoms, Necco wafers, molasses kisses, besides chocolate creams and gumdrops. His ice-cream tins had been dumped out of their ice chest and had lost their covers. They had seen whole gallons of strawberry, vanilla, and chocolate beginning to melt around the edges and run into each other. It was a sight so impressive that no one had a word to say until one of the older boys tried the door handle and then there was a breathless waiting. But it would not give. It was either locked or jammed hard.

"Suppose I heave a rock?" said Jim Gunley, looking sideways at the girls to see how they would take it.

"A lot of good that would do," said the older boy, whom they did not know, "getting the eats full of glass."

Perhaps they had had good dinners somehow, in the middle of the storm. Anyway the villagers began to leave except some quite small ones who could not take their noses off the glass. Jim Gunley went when someone came up with a story that a dead man had been washed up below Olsen's boathouse.

"Do you want to see him?" asked Jane.

"Not much," said Edie. "I'd rather have some ice cream, wouldn't you?"

"Well," said Jane, "there doesn't look like much hope of that either." She wondered what Edie expected. Even if all Mr. Lumsden's doors burst open, they couldn't just take his things. They couldn't even take them if they fell out on the dirt.

"I'm going home," she said.

"Wait just precisely three and a half minutes more," said Edie. "Mr. Lumsden might come himself."

"He won't. He's gone to Far's Landing. I heard Mr. Olsen saying so."

But Edie had to circle the parlor as if she were a beagle, and Jane had to follow at her heels to be sure she did not do anything to get put in jail. And she had to listen to her arguments too. Edie thought Mr. Lumsden might have been drowned in the storm or hit by a tree in Far's Landing. Then the ice-cream parlor wouldn't belong to anybody.

"Yes, it would," said Jane. "He'd have left it to a relation in his will. Edie, you can't do anything. I won't let you. It would be stealing."

"I just want to *see*," said Edie.

She fiddled with the upside-down latch of the back door.

"The boys have tried that already," said Jane. "I saw

them." This, she made up. But it was better to tell a few lies at the moment, she thought.

Edie put her eye to the keyhole. "I bet it isn't locked," she said. "Come on, scare cat, let's give it one little tug."

Jane would have nothing to do with it. The small children had come round from the front and were standing behind them in a row, looking with all their might. She knew very well that if anything startling happened, some one of them would go off to get his mother and she and Edie would be caught for burglars. She put out her hand to catch Edie's hard brown wrist that was going toward the latch when there was a tug at her skirt. It was Jim Gunley's younger brother who had taken his thumb out of his mouth and was trying to say something. *"What?"* said Jane, leaning over to try to hear the whisper. "Wait, Edie, wait," she said, holding her. "I think he's saying he heard a noise. Where?" said Jane to Harold Gunley. Harold pointed at Mr. Lumsden's back door.

"What did I tell you!" said Edie.

Jane reluctantly put her finger on the foolish, weak-looking latch, and Edie grasped above it with her whole tough brown hand. "Pull!" she said. The door gave a rasping scratch and opened a few inches. "See!"

She tried to peek through the crack, but it was too dark to see anything, or else there was something in the way. They both took hold of the edge and jerked, and the door gave onto the tiny passage where Mr. Lumsden kept boxes, papers, a garbage pail, and his broom. They were all there in a heap upside down with boards, sticks, and dirt on top, and on top of *them* were a pair of men's boots, which must have been on the floor and got flung up there when the house went over.

When the door was opened, the pile of rubbish began to fall out and Jane did not like it. "Now you've done it," she said. But Edie was staring at the boots, and she stared too when she saw what was happening. The boxes fell at their feet, but the boots stayed up in the air. They had legs attached to them! These kept stiff for a minute and then, as more stuff loosened and fell, they began to waver and fall too.

"It's a live man," said Edie, scrabbling at the boxes.

"It's a dead man," said Jane. "I wish you'd mind your own business once in a while." But she helped with hauling things away from the legs, and except for a wooden crate that they had a hard time getting away from where it was wedged against the doorjamb, they were very quick about it, and very careful to keep out of the way of the legs, which now stretched out beside them. Edie finally got a stone out of the back lot to break up the crate, and at a last mighty tug it came away and they sat down on the step outside the sill and also on their audience, which had moved up as close as possible to get the best view. Two of them ran off screaming, just as Jane had been sure they would.

"It's their own fault," said Edie. "Come on. Let's see what's happened."

They crawled back on their hands and knees in order not to run into the legs, but they were gone, and there at the end of the dark passage sat Mr. Lumsden in a white apron, blinking at them. Jane and Edie sank back on their heels and they all looked at each other quite a while.

"Quite a blow," said Mr. Lumsden. "It tipped me over."

"I hope you're still alive," said Jane politely.

"Gut rush uv blood to the head," said Mr. Lumsden. "Bin on it an hour or more." He shook his head violently as if trying to clear it. "Shouldn't wonder you saved me."

"Oh no!" said Jane modestly, thinking of what they had thought about the candy and ice cream.

"We *did,* more or *less,*" said Edie. Jane gave her a look. "We were trying to save your store and we found you."

"I'm lucky," said Mr. Lumsden.

He got up and stood swaying from side to side and trying to clear his vision by waving cobwebs away from before his face. Presently he stepped out on the grass. "Upside down," he said, considering the ice-cream parlor, "plum upside down."

"Almost everything has spilled," said Edie. "Would you like to see it?"

They guided him, still weaving, to the plate-glass window.

"Them boxes," he said, feeling himself and flexing his legs, "plum jammed me in."

His look in his big window did not seem to inspire him with thoughts of any kind at all; it just made him continue to shake his head. Edie, and even Jane, was more than surprised; they were both disappointed and impatient that Mr. Lumsden, whom they had saved, with that ocean of candy and ice cream in front of him, useless as far as selling was concerned, beginning to melt already, with syrups creeping nearer and nearer to bars of Peter's chocolate, and dirt and dust dropping all over it from what used to be the floor—

Mr. Lumsden did not have an inkling of the right thing to do.

"Goodness," he said. "Goodness."

"It'll be badness pretty soon," said Edie. With Jane listening she did not dare be any fresher than that.

But he did not catch on, and they finally had to leave him walking unsteadily round and round the ice-cream parlor followed by that part of the audience that had dared to remain, wondering how he could get it right side up again.

"Wouldn't you have thought," said Edie, stepping over a crevasse that the water had made in the road back to Aunt Louise's, "that he could just have offered us a package of Neccos for saving his life!"

"It was just an accident," said Jane.

"For you, but not for me," said Edie, wagging her head. "You know *that*."

They got back to Aunt Louise's just in time to see Hubert and Ted sculling across the harbor with some of the furniture tied behind the skiff like dead whales; and just in time for an enormous supper that Cook had somehow invented from what had been on the top kitchen shelves. Gander served it in her rubbers. And just in time to see that the boat that was still looking in their front door was still unoccupied by Shaw Wells; and just in time to be able to get to bed before they fell down. Edie sat for two minutes with her arms to hold her up, her short yellow hair dripping backwards.

"Gee, Jane," she said, while Widgy who was curled up at the foot of the bed looked at her with one eye, "I wish every day could be like this one, don't you?"

CHAPTER FIVE

The Enemy

Waking up at Aunt Louise's was almost always a good sensation, no matter what kind of day it might be, because of the sounds that the wind, light or strong, brought in before your eyes were even open. There was particularly the clock chunk of boats and the chuck, chuck, chuck of Captain Grannet's lobster launch setting out steadily and firmly to visit the pots. These made you part of everything to do with salt water, so that you saw the wet piles of the wharfs at low tide, barnacles, mud flats or the brimming harbor, quahogs under boulders, scurrying fiddler crabs, and screaming gulls. In between these noises the pine trees soughed and breathed through the window until you were ready to get up and see what kind of a day it was—the kind when you went swimming on the outer beach and ducked through the surf, or the kind when you dived for clam shells from the float, or the kind that you spent entirely on getting ready to race and fixing things up after you had.

The morning after the "big blow" there was not a sound. The sun was streaming in and the air was stirring as usual, but the wind seemed to have blown away even the wonderful beach smells. Edie woke up knowing that it was going to be an exciting day—everything would have to be cleaned up as if it were the beginning of the world—even in her sleep she had been looking forward to it. She, personally, meant to rescue the player piano, investigate Shaw Wells's sloop, help bail the *Q,* and see if any of those mice had come to life—there would be a thousand things she liked, and therefore when she lay in bed listening and heard none of them beginning, she sat up startled with surprise. The only sound was the ticking of the window shade cord. Except for that there were no inside noises either. Usually there was Lou who came in to say: "Mith-thes, are you awake?" and poked her finger in your eye to see if you were, and Theodore tramping and Hubert blowing his nose and Gander sounding as if an elephant had got hold of a dustpan. She remembered that Lou and Chris and Mr. Parker were still away, but what about the others? And the smell of breakfast? The blow should not have done anything to that. Aunt Louise's great iron stove was on a brick platform, and the water had only licked its feet; also the part-time man had been *glad* to spite the electricity so that he could set up the old gasoline pump in the cellar last night. She had seen it working herself. It was not strong enough to get a bath from its workings, but it could have sent coffee water into the kitchen, she was sure, and with just a little wood from the wood pile, which had a small roof of its own, there should have been bacon. Somewhere, somehow, she began to realize, life must be going on without her and she had better get up and see. As she stepped to the floor, no little dog jumped down beside her.

"Why, Widgy, bad dog, where are you?" she said. How *could* he have gone off without her?

One of the best things about summer was how easy it was to get dressed; stretch your legs twice for pants, throw a dress over your head, pull on some socks, put your feet into sneakers, and that was it until Mr. Parker or Theodore saw you. Then maybe you had to wash your face if they thought of it, which honestly did seem rather foolish when you were in water most of the time. This morning especially she felt that she had had enough of it yesterday and took no pains to be any cleaner than when she went to bed. Now that her hair was short, a comb did whatever was necessary in "a brace of lightning shakes" exactly as the part-time man said he would do things. She was downstairs in three and a half minutes, and it took her much less to discover why Aunt Louise's was so quiet. There was no one in the house but herself, not even in the kitchen, not a sight or a sound of a soul. She had overslept, she saw by the kitchen clock, and she bet as she came back to the hall that they had all gone off to see some marvelous sight without her. It must have promised to be extra marvelous because they had left breakfast scattered all over the table without clearing off a thing. It was probably that dead man that she and Jane had heard about in the village, or the white yacht that the boys had reported last night had gone on the rocks in the narrows. What a party of skunks to leave her out of it when they knew perfectly well that she was the one person in the family who didn't mind getting up early! And where was Widgy? She really did not see how Widgy could have deserted her. He had never been mean in the whole of his life. That riddle, however, was soon solved. They had shut him in the downstairs toilet room—to be out of their way, she supposed. Now he welcomed her as if she had saved his life, going crazy and running in circles and making noises in his throat.

"Where are they, Widge? Show me where they are," said Edie, but he only talked louder and said nothing. Anyway he was only interested in her. That was some consolation.

Edie went into the dining room and ate some pieces of bacon that had gotten soft and cold. Couldn't even *Cook* have stayed at home—the fat old thing. How could she go anywhere with her kind of feet? She spread butter and jam on soft cold toast, drank a glass of milk down in one long series of swallowings, and went out through the side veranda door. She was glad to see the sloop was still there. Someone had moved the top of the pine tree that had settled beyond it, but luckily you could not move sloops across dry land as quickly as that. And there was still no one in it as she found out by hallooing to see who would come up from the cabin. As soon as she had seen about the mice and fed Jocko and Laza who were living in the barn, she would come back and get aboard herself. She had always been dying to see Shaw Wells's sloop.

At the boathouse she felt too sad to stay. The mice were certainly dead and looked terrible. She dropped them into the bushes as Hubert had suggested. The player piano was still full of water and it was too heavy for her to tip over; every single roll was drenched through, and the top of the boathouse was still standing on end against the trees behind it. Wouldn't you think they'd be doing something about something, she said to herself, as she decided to take a look out the balcony window, hoping there might be somebody in sight on the beach. There wasn't, not even somebody towing a rescued boat out or bailing a sunk skiff. In the stable the animals were all right and very hungry, so she gave them what she had brought and listened dejectedly as they scolded her. The Ford was all right too, but she was rather disgusted with it and gave it a kick for being so undisturbed. She wandered up the shell road to see if she could see somebody or something from the bridge that went over the railroad tracks. Hooray! There was a man there. It was awfully funny, because the part-time man didn't come till the afternoon, but probably it was somebody from the railroad.

"Jumping beans!" said Edie softly as she came nearer and could see clearer. "It's a man with a gun."

Not only that, but he had on a uniform like a soldier. It *was* a soldier. She went on so that she could really inspect him, and hearing the crunching on the shell road, the soldier raised his head and began to inspect her. Right away he stepped into the middle of the bridge and shifted his gun to the ready.

"You can't cross here," he said.

"Why not?" said Edie.

"Regulations," said the soldier.

"Is there a war?" said Edie, trying to be funny.

"Are you kidding?" said the soldier.

"No, I just wanted to know."

"Look," said the soldier, "you run along home." He made a sort of stabbing movement with his gun. "I'm guarding this bridge, see."

"It's our bridge," said Edie. "I *live* here."

"I don't care about that," said the soldier. "Right now this bridge is under the protection of the United States Militia, so make yourself scarce, sister."

"Then there *is* a war?" said Edie seriously. She was beginning to think there must be.

"Can I just look over the bridge?"

"You can't do nothing but go back where you come from," said the soldier and put his gun out to keep her from making a step forward.

Edie hated to turn back because she had been ordered to by a fresh soldier, she hated it so much that she lifted one of her feet to—

"Oh no you don't," said the soldier, and Edie found herself sitting on the shell road not quite sure how she got there. It was so uncomfortable she got up at once.

"All right for you," she said, but she didn't know what she meant by it. She was sure she would never be able to get Theodore or Hubert to get into a fight over her, especially not with a man who had a gun, and more especially not with the United States Army. Who could the army be fighting? Well, just to get the better of him for that rude trick, she would get a look down the railroad in spite of him. And she knew a way through the sweet pea garden at the back of Aunt Louise's little woods. She had never thought of it before, but Aunt Louise's house and all the houses in a line with it were on a sort of island, one side bordered by the tracks that went down for miles to the very end of the beach and the other side bordered by the harbor. It might be that everybody on this side was being protected in some way from the enemy.

Edie went through the woods, opened the gate to the garden, and was out on the slope above the tracks in a very few minutes. Crickets! There was another soldier below her, and still another beyond him. She moved quickly back into the trees, but her soldier had seen her and began shouting, and the one on the tracks shouted as well. It made such a commotion that she was embarrassed and decided to make herself scarce as she had been told to do. Anyway, if she couldn't go that way, she could still go by the shore to see if she could find somebody. Was it another Civil War, she asked herself? And how did it begin so quickly? It might be a good thing to be guarded, but why did they have to make you feel as if you were the enemy yourself?

"Come on, Widge," she said. "Let's go down to the shore."

Widgy was only too glad to go anywhere. He followed right at her heels with his face almost on her sneakers and his tongue hanging out.

She took the path down the ravine by the boathouse across which she had had to swim yesterday. It was rather a mess because the water had tangled the bushes and mixed in some sticks and a whole lot of seaweed and sand, but she resolutely pushed her way through, particularly the last part where the blueberry bushes met across the path. As she stumbled headlong out, she almost fell into the lap of a soldier who was taking it easy on a crate that the tide had washed up. He jumped to his feet and held his gun across her just like the first one.

"Can't come down here today, sister," he said.

"Will you please tell me why *not*," said Edie. "This is *our* beach. At least it's our aunt's."

"Regulations," said the soldier.

"Where can I go?"

"If I was you," said the soldier, "I'd go home."

"There's nobody there."

"Are you lost, sister?"

"I said," said Edie speaking louder, "there—is—nobody —in—my—house. I'm trying to find them."

"Sounds kind of suspicious to me," said the soldier. "Where they gone?"

In all her life, Edie thought, she had never met so many stupid, nutty men at one time. And here she was, left all alone to be guarded by them in time of war. Had everybody run away? Or had they been captured? Or what? She gathered her muscles together to be as polite and clear as she possibly could.

"I wouldn't be looking for them if I knew where they were," she said as gently and calmly as she could make her voice sound. Then she gathered herself in still more. "Could you *please,* if you don't mind, *sir,* tell me—*are* we having a war?"

"Why sure," said the soldier, dropping the butt of his gun to the sand and grinning. "I thought you knew, lady."

He waited for Edie to go back through the blueberry bushes, but she still stood there. She had so many questions she wanted to ask, she could only think of one.

"Where's my family? That's what I'd like to know."

"Maybe they're arrested," said the soldier casually.

"What for?"

"Darned if I know. Say, you better get along. I'm supposed to be patrolling this beach not answering kid questions all day long."

"Just let me walk down the shore to the path," she said. "The bushes are too thick right there."

"Cheese it, then," said the soldier, "and don't forget I have my eye on you neither."

Edie started down the sand. She meant to be as honorable and obedient as the United States Militia required, since they were here for her protection, but she had not gone two steps before she saw a figure down the sand that she could tell was Theodore because he had on Father's yachting cap that Father had told him not to wear. She did not mean to, but the sight simply *made* her run, and she seemed to know while she was doing it that it was much easier in sneakers than in boots and with a gun.

"Hey, Ted," she called, stopping, so that her voice would have all its strength. "Hey, wait!" And then she ran on.

Edie was never sure whether the soldier fired off his gun and scared her or whether she just tripped over a stone. Anyway there seemed to be a terrible noise and she fell flat. Widgy bounded about her head, licking wherever he could find a place. "I can still move," she thought, "so I'm not dead." And she would have started on again, but she ran into a pair of legs.

Oh my goodness, a *thousand* jumping beans! It was just another soldier. What she had thought was Father's yachting cap was an officer's hat. Well, she hadn't done anything but run, and they couldn't make her say she had. There wasn't any law against running, she was pretty sure.

But apparently in wartime there was. The officer took her arm. "Little girl," he said, "you're not allowed here today. Go home."

"Let go of my arm first."

The officer still held on.

"I can kick."

"Kick away."

If she hadn't known what men thought about people for crying, she could have cried with rage. An officer ought to have some sense.

"Well," she said, "I *am* going home. See that path there? But let go of my arm."

The officer let her arm drop and stepped back. Edie skinned past him up the path that led to the piazza steps. When she was out of reach, she stopped and turned round.

"I haven't done a thing," she said. "I'm merely looking for my family. *And,*" she added a little out of breath, "you might tell a person what you're doing on their aunt's property."

"We're protecting your aunt's property," the officer called back and turned away.

Edie went up the rest of the path slowly. So there was a war and this strip of land was being patrolled on both sides. She supposed she ought to be grateful, but she thought she had never in all her born days met such irritating people as there were in the United States Militia.

When she got back to the house, it was just as she had left it, just as empty and silent and full of dirt and green slime, and the breakfast table still had some pieces of cold bacon and cold toast. She finished them up, giving Widgy half of each very fairly, while she listened to the silence and tried to think. Maybe she better start making some barricades. It was what people usually did in a war. But she saw right away that that was silly. Anybody could get into Aunt Louise's anywhere. That was something she had always liked about it, and it was no use pretending she could take care of all the doors and windows all alone. What then? Certainly if the others had all somehow gotten themselves captured and only she was left, she ought to be doing something to help out the army whether they wanted her or not. Susan would be sure to say that any Southerner could have done it.

By the time she and Widgy had finished the toast and had almost finished chewing, she had thought of the very thing. She would go up to the passage that led to the cupola —"I mean where the cupola used to be," she said to herself —and lock herself in. Then she could open the trap door and take up a station there to watch what was going on. She would be able to see a great deal better than any of the soldiers; she would be able to see everything all up and down the beach. When the enemy approached, she would be able to see *them* and she could either give a terrific shriek from the roof or dash down and warn that officer in time. It was a perfect idea, she thought, and she only hoped those dumb militias would have the sense to pay attention. It was such a good idea that she would get started on it right now.

In spite of Edie's enthusiasm she was relieved when the screen door slammed just as she was going upstairs from the second landing with Widgy lolloping softly after her. A million times hooray, she thought. She never would have expected to be so glad to see Theodore and Hubert, and even Jane. And maybe Mr. Parker had come back with Hood and the children. She leaned over the rail to see—and froze.

It wasn't any of them. It wasn't a soldier either, at least he
didn't have a uniform, but it was another man with a gun,
a short one, a pistol, held out in front of him as if he would
be ready to shoot any minute. Edie pulled back her head. It
was the enemy! There was no doubt about that. He *looked*
like the enemy, no matter what Susan Stoningham said
about their being handsome, and he had walked right in as
if he knew there was nobody at home, or didn't care. How
could the Civil War possibly have begun again? Even Mr.
Parker who read the newspapers hadn't said a word about
it, but she could hear china rattling and breaking as if he
was in a fury because there was no food, just the way the
enemy was supposed to. Next he would be coming upstairs.
She flitted softly up to the third floor and looked over. Yup,
he was coming, but he stopped to investigate the rooms on
the second floor. In the boys' room he made a kind of rumpus
and talked to himself.

"Nothing but runts!" she heard him say.

It was true that Ted was a lot smaller than he was.
He probably wanted to change clothes and look like some
other man. But the United States, she thought, getting more
frightened, must be fighting somebody perfectly terrible
this time because in all the books she had read the men in
gray had been full of old-fashioned courtesy, taking what
they had to take and saluting the lady of the house as they
rode away. This guy had smashed Aunt Louise's china and
called the family names. Edie suddenly became quite sure
that it was time to get out of his way altogether.

There was nowhere to go but the stairs to the roof, but
she remembered her plan and let herself into their darkness

quietly, switching the key to the inside and turning it with care. She waited a minute to try to soothe Widgy who was jumping about in her arms. No dog likes to have his mouth held together, naturally, and she didn't blame him. She could hear the enemy coming up the next flight and almost shook for the time when he would see her door and try to get it open. It came pretty soon, and when he found it locked, he kicked it and swore. Probably he would have liked to get to the roof himself and see what the army was doing. To Edie, it seemed as if he might pull or push the door down any minute, so that with her noiseless sneakers she went noiselessly up the stairs to get the trap door open. Someone had closed it after the storm, of course.

"It's life or death," she kept saying, "it's life or death, so you better do it right."

The trap door was heavy, much too heavy to lift with one hand. She would have to put Widgy down; there was nothing else to do. "If you'd only keep quiet," she said to him, "it will only take a sec." And for a sec he did sit quietly shivering beside her, but when the door was rattled again, it was too much for him and he threw himself down the stairs in a craziness of barking. Now, she knew, she had to get onto that roof quick. She put her shoulders under the trap door and lifted with all her might. It moved up and she followed it up a step and then another, and when she could get an arm through, pulled a piece of broken wood from the cupola into the crack to make a wedge. Widgy tore back up the stairs and out the opening and barked wildly from the roof, but Edie could now use her back, and forcing the door upright was not so hard. With all Widgy's racket she now had no idea what the enemy might be doing. If she shut the door again and sat on it, he could easily toss her off, so that would be a waste of time. Instead she steadied herself and filled her lungs to give the loudest scream that had ever been heard. The Lord only knew whether those foolish militias would do anything about it, but it was life or death.

Just as she opened her mouth, she saw it wasn't necessary. Widgy had done it instead. "Good Widge," she said, patting him over and over. She did not like it, but her voice and hand trembled a little. "Good, good, Widge." The enemy was sneaking along the blueberry bushes toward the ravine and the boathouse, keeping his head below them. She watched him go crouching along, without even time to look back, and then when he got to the boathouse standing upright and disappearing, just as if he knew the narrow path there, into the tangle of bushes at the side of the stable. Now she knew exactly what to do. Not scream and let him know there was a person around as well as a dog, but get down to the shore as fast as she could and tell those dumb soldiers. She skithered to the bottom of the three flights of stairs, hurled herself down the piazza steps, and raced for the beach. She hoped the militias were still there! As she ran, she had a frightful thought for the first time. If one of these enemies had broken through there might be a whole lot more of them. Would the militias be able to take care of them? Well, if she was going to be captured or killed, she wouldn't be it all alone. It seemed to make a difference, so that she could run faster. When she reached the sand, she stopped, looking wildly to right and left to see which way to go. "Oh blessed day," she thought, just like Cook; the officer was sitting on the dry end of what was left of the pier swinging his legs and tapping his boots with a short stick. He got up the minute he saw her and began moving the stick up and down. Edie was too blown to run through the loose sand, so she waited, panting.

"I thought I told you—" the officer began.

"They're here," said Edie, without much breath. "They're in my house."

"Who?" asked the officer sternly.

"The enemy," said Edie, still panting and then swallowing. "At least one of them is. There might be more by this time. You better get your men together."

"What enemy?" said the officer, doing nothing at all but look at her. "Little girl, I told you to go home and play dolls, not soldiers."

It was a hopeless world, grownups were hopeless, men were hopeless, and soldiers were so hopeless that she wondered how America ever won the Revolution. Still, this was so important she would have to try again.

"I *went* home," she said, trying to make things simple and clear so that this hopeless militia would understand. "I went home like you said, but while I was there, one of the enemy got through somehow and he's changed his clothes— at least he did partly—and he tried to take some food, but there wasn't any." She couldn't keep it up. "My family's been captured," she yelled at him. "If there's a war, aren't you supposed to FIGHT? Are you just stupid or COWARDS or WHAT?"

In all her life she would never believe in the militias again. Susan Stoningham was right. Although the enemy hadn't been handsome or polite, at least he knew what to do when there was a war. This officer was still just standing there. The enemy was probably miles away by this time, if he hadn't just gone back to tell his army it was the right time to attack.

"Well," she said discouraged, "it's all over by now."

"What is?" said the officer, frowning. "I see you're in a tizzy about something, but I don't know what you're talking about. Of course we fight in a war, but what's that got to do with it? Are you all right in the head?"

"Will you kindly tell me just ONE THING," said Edie finally, after staring at him. "If you will, I'll do anything you say."

"Sure," said the officer.

"Is—there—a—war?"

"No," said the officer, "of course not."

"Then, *what*—are—you—doing—here?"

"We're here to stop looting," said the officer.

"What's that?"

"Stealing—good heavens! There's been a hurricane and everything's wide open. Didn't you know it?"

"A hurricane!" said Edie. "I thought it was just a big blow. I was in it," she added modestly. "But then," she said, looking out at the water thoughtfully, "if that man wasn't the enemy, he was a burglar."

"Good heavens!" said the officer again. He turned sharply and reached in his pocket. "Good holy heavens! Why didn't you say so?" He put a whistle to his mouth and blew it sharply and hard. Whistles began blowing all up and down the shore.

"Where did you say he had gone?" the officer asked.

"I'll show you," said Edie.

"At the double, men," said the officer. "This young lady thinks she's seen what we're looking for."

Edie and Widgy at the double led the soldiers back up the piazza steps to the lawn where they very nearly ran over her family as it came round the corner the opposite way.

"Cripes!" said Theodore, as the Militia swept by. "We needn't have worried about *her*. She's got the whole United States Army looking after her."

"I'll be back in a minute," yelled Edie. "Where *have* you been?"

She led the soldiers to the edge of the tangled bushes by the stable and showed them the tiny path that led through them. "He went in there. But you better look out. He's armed, and he *might* have friends." She felt she should give them all the advice she could, considering what kind of brains they had, and she hoped fervently that that officer really knew what he was talking about and just had not *heard* about a war.

To her disgust the soldiers again only stood looking while Theodore and Hubert and Jane stood in a knot on the veranda waiting to see how she was going to manage things.

"That ain't no place to get caught in," said one soldier. "Shoot us down like flies."

"No, it ain't at that," said another, feeling his chin.

But the officer blew his whistle again and gave orders. "Surround this patch of bushes," he said. "Get going!" The soldiers trotted off to right and left, and the officer stayed at the entrance to the path. "Sergeant, you go down by the beach and alert that bunch at the other end."

Edie, while she waited, had a sudden belated thought.

"But what's he done?" she asked. "You never told me what he'd done. He didn't take anything from Aunt Louise's." You really couldn't count a pair of Theodore's old pants.

"Little girl," said the officer, "go home now and sell your papers. You've given us a good lead and we thank you, but it's dangerous here." He looked her in the eye. "And take your dog with you. He might get stepped on."

Edie started walking backwards under his look. She really hated going back to Aunt Louise's and to her old family who had probably only been down to the village after all. That burglar was hers! At least she ought to be told what he had done. She was worried about it. It was terrible to have to think that she had arranged to have somebody put in jail when he hadn't done anything but try to take Theodore's pants, when he wasn't even the enemy.

"Ted, what did he *do?* That's what I want to know. Why don't you answer? Where have you guys been anyway? I might be dead by this time."

"Not you," said Theodore.

"We've been under arrest, cock-eye, if you want to know," said Hubert.

"I might have known you'd do something to get arrested for," said Edie. "But if you'd be so condescending as to explain the smallest thing—" She pushed past them hurriedly and went up to her room where she slammed the door behind her and flung herself across the bed. If she had had a man caught and jailed, electrocuted for all she knew, she would never get over it for the rest of her life. Those militias were stupid enough to do anything.

It was not long before Jane knocked, and she had to sit up quickly on the edge of the bed to show there was nothing the matter. Theodore and Hubert sat down on the other bed and Jane wandered around. They had come, they said politely, to tell her what had been going on, if she felt in the mood to hear. Edie nodded.

What had happened was that there had been a big hullabaloo over at fat Mrs. Johnson's next door while they were in the middle of breakfast. She, Edie, must have been dead drunk asleep not to have heard it. And naturally they had gone to see what was up. They had only meant to be gone a minute.

"Cook and Gander *too?*" asked Edie.

"They're still there," said Jane, "under suspicion."

"And so were we," said Hubert, "until ten minutes ago. I must say soldiers have awfully little judgment."

"That's what I think," said Edie.

Well, when they got there, all the doors at Mrs. Johnson's had been wide open, so they walked in, and there was nobody there. The hullabaloo had gone off somewhere else. Cook and Gander, once on the scent, had followed it apparently because they were brought back pretty soon with a soldier on each arm. They were shoved in the door, and one of the soldiers had asked Ted if those females belonged to him.

"And he said—" said Jane.

"And I said," said Theodore, getting up and pacing up and down like Jane.

"He said 'God forbid,' " said Jane very quickly.

"I also said I would take care of them for a while if he so desired."

"And then the soldier said he'd take care of them and us too," said Hubert.

Ted had argued with the soldier. "Quite reasonably for him," said Jane, and told him just how they got there and why, but it did no good. He had his orders and "in the army, kid," he said, "you do what you're told."

"I bet he hadn't been told to give Cook a poke with his gun butt," said Hubert.

"Well, it shut her up."

But not Gander—you couldn't shut her up if the sky was coming down. *She* said: "If you touch me with your filthy weapons, young man, you'll be the worse for it."

"So I'm filthy, am I?" said the soldier. "All right, you're all under arrest."

"But what *for*," said Edie, rocking back and forth. "You never say what *for*."

"For fat Mrs. Johnson's fat jewelry," said Hubert, lying back on the bed and yawning. "Somebody took it. By the way, did you know we'd had a hurricane?"

They had had to stay there for hours while the soldier leaned against the wall with his hat on the back of his head. He said he was waiting for orders.

"Mrs. Johnson's house is not as bad as ours," said Jane.

"Just the same she went to stay at her brother's, leaving her jewills behind her," said Hubert.

"Who took them?"

"You're the only one who knows, sweetheart," said Theodore. "How about telling us."

She was? How? When did she ever see anybody taking jewels? Oh my, said Edie's mind. Of course. It was the Enemy. That man. He probably had them in his pocket right then and he had come into Aunt Louise's because he knew nobody was there. He had come to change his clothes, get something to eat, and get away. Widgy had foiled him!

She told them about it and they listened respectfully. Even Theodore said: "Ck—ck," every so often and pounded his fists together. On account of this and their respectfulness, she left out the part about the boys being runts. She was almost sure they would not like it.

"Too bad you couldn't have shut him in somewhere. *That* would have showed 'em," said Ted at the end.

"Well, he was a whole lot bigger than me," said Edie apologetically.

Finally they had to stop talking—no, not stop, but anyway go downstairs and see about cleaning up the house. Gander had said flatly that she could not do it alone, no, not even after she got out of the hands of "them doughfaces." It was too much for her entirely, and as they could not go anywhere, it didn't seem a bad thing to do. Besides, last night the boys had towed back from across the harbor quite a few pieces of Aunt Louise's furniture, and because it was soaked with salt water, it would have to be drenched down with the hose. A delightful job. Which, of course, was undertaken by the boys simply because it was no use

Jane and Edie thinking they could get the hose away from them.

"It'll never regain its pristine beauty," said Hubert sadly, when it was set up on the lawn and he and Ted were in their bathing suits hopping around and sprinkling each other, "but we'll do what we can."

Jane and Edie reminded them, before they went to get mops and pails, about the gasoline pump and no bath water, but they only answered: "All the better for you, my dears, you won't have to wash."

Just the same they worked very hard all the rest of the morning, and themselves sloshed a good deal of water pleasantly through the parlor and wicker chair room, in the end sweeping it out the door and letting the boys run it off the veranda boards. Their knees got sore crawling along and wiping the baseboards, and they said to each other that they bet a lot of the dirt was much older than the hurricane. Edie heard all the news there was to hear. That Mrs. Johnson had come back from her brother's and they were released and shown the house and what had happened to it, which wasn't very bad, and the very place where the jewels had been taken from, a real safe in the dining room. "So somebody must have known the combination," said Jane.

"Who?" said Edie.

"How do I know," said Jane. "Mrs. Johnson *said* she kept it in her head, so I don't suppose anybody could get it out of there without an operation."

"Very funny!" said Edie. "Do you think they'll catch that man, Jane?"

"Probably they will," said Jane, getting up and trying to straighten out. "Come on. That's good enough. Let's see if we're going to get any lunch."

Gander was just coming in to tell them that they were. "But you're to go to the lady yonder for your dinners this night," she added. "Cook's all asthray," even though Mrs. Johnson, she told them, had finally convinced the army they were not thieves.

"What about *her* cook?" asked Jane.

"Sure her help's all come back to her," said Gander, "after being scattered like hens from the fright. And the butler himself down on his knees with his coat off scrubbing with the best of them. I never thought I'd see the day."

"Look what *we've* done," said Edie. "You might appreciate it."

"Save us and bless us," said Gander. " 'Tis one miracle after the other and no mistake."

As for themselves, they stayed dirty the whole day. Such a tremendous cleaning would have to be done for Mrs. Johnson's dinner that it seemed foolish to do anything beforehand. Even Theodore, who was getting so that he prinked quite a lot, especially for Mrs. Palmer, was "a sight to be'old" as Hood was always saying about the children. They ate standing up, just because it was a waste of time to sit down, and every once in a while they sent a scout into the outside world. When it was Hubert, he said when he came back: "I think the guy got away. All those rookies are back where they were, and just as fresh as ever. Otherwise the dove of peace has descended on the world."

It seemed too bad to spend the last lovely evening they

would have without Mr. Parker or Hood or the children all dressed up at fat Mrs. Johnson's, but Hubert remarked about six o'clock that he would sell his birthright for a mess of pottage any time, only he hoped it was going to be a good one. Gander very kindly brought out some hot buttered toast and tea about four, but that was worked off in no time hanging the damp rolls of the player piano on the blueberry bushes. Theodore, when he at last had time to think about it, thought they might be saved. Edie had worked desperately.

"You really are a sight, Edith," said her brother kindly. "You better leave time to hang *yourself* out somewhere for a while."

Edie didn't care what he said at all. She was sure that the player piano was going to be all right again. Quite easily she could let the mice go. There would probably very soon be some more. And anyway, she thought, Ted might have taken his own advice when she saw how he looked to go to Mrs. Johnson's. There were separate drops of water on every hair at the back of his neck.

Fat Mrs. Johnson was on the harbor-side terrace to greet them because she had been watching the white yacht that had been blown on the rocks in the narrows. It seemed to her strange that no one was doing anything about it. They had to make conversation with her so long that Hubert tightened his belt.

"I just thought I'd give her a hint," he said later.

She didn't take it, however. Even after the butler had come out and announced dinner behind their backs, they had to stand there and keep wondering about the white yacht. "Just as if," said Theodore, "it hadn't been her who sent for the army and kept us all from doing anything in the first place." His own boat, he wished them to observe, was still under water.

It was Edie who managed to stop her.

"We've got a sloop on our lawn," she said. "It's almost in the front door."

"Imagine!" said Mrs. Johnson. "Don't let her sloop you, my dear."

They all said "Ha, ha," out of positive gratitude, because she turned at last and led the way into the dining room. Once there, they could enjoy themselves, even for a short while without any food, because they could always be sure that her dining table would be quite a wonder, and this time in spite of everything it was the same. How did she do it? All the fruit in the middle was real and so were the nasturtiums in little vases at the four corners. They had been out to look at Aunt Louise's sweet pea garden, and every blossom had been torn to shreds. It added so much to the questions they wanted to ask that they felt stifled while the maid brought in the soup and Mrs. Johnson told them that the white yacht on the rocks, she *thought,* belonged to some people called White. "Quite a coincidence, isn't it?"

"Believe you and me," said Theodore enthusiastically. "Mrs. Johnson," he said louder than usual before she could begin again, "how did you manage to save all your stuff? Ours went right across the harbor."

"My new James," said Mrs. Johnson. "That's my butler, my dear. My wonderful new James. He stayed right here and hung onto the door."

"Your water couldn't have been as high as ours," said Edie, putting down her soup spoon. "Ours *smashed* the door."

"He says it was very high," said Mrs. Johnson, "and you're sitting on the furniture this minute. I don't think you were here to see what he did," she added severely, stretching her stoutness, "so perhaps you'll believe your elders."

Theodore nudged Edie and Hubert kicked her under the table to make her shut up and not argue with a hostess, but she did not like it, so she looked down hard at her place while the wonderful new James changed the plates.

"Would you tell us about your jewels, Mrs. Johnson," said Jane politely, trying to break the uncomfortable silence.

"Hush, my dear," said Mrs. Johnson, "do hush." She put her finger to her lips. "Everyone's so sensitive, you know. James," she said, as the butler came into the room again, "show these young people how you held the door."

"Certainly, Madam," said James as he put the chicken on a side table. "It was like this, Madam, with the waves beating on the outside." He went to the glass door, bolted it, and stood with his knee and foot pressed hard against it. They all watched his back and saw the muscles standing out under his butler's coat. They had to believe he had done it all right. Edie watched particularly, thinking he must be a marvelous kind of man. Why hadn't Theodore and Hubert thought of that? She sat with her head down in to her shoulders with admiration.

"That's how it was, Madam," said James, turning to face them.

Edie spent one more second with her head in her

shoulders. Then she sat up, but something told her to do it slowly. This man was the Enemy! She knew it as plain as day. Mrs. Johnson's wonderful new James was *the Enemy*. Was she going crazy? Maybe he had a twin brother or something. When he passed her the chicken, she dropped the serving spoon and it went clattering to the floor. As he picked it up, the long dark hair that she had seen fell over his forehead and he had to put it back with two fingers. She had seen him do that too. It was the same man all right and his gun would be in his pocket. She was going to have to be awfully, awfully careful.

Edie's being so careful completely took away her power of eating, and as fat Mrs. Johnson liked everybody to eat including herself, she began to fuss.

"The child's stomach must be out of order," she said. "Can't you eat all that good food, my dear?"

Edie took some of everything and tried putting it in in little bits, but with the Enemy stirring round the dining room her throat would not swallow. *What* was she going to do? Should she yell? Mrs. Johnson wouldn't believe her and the Enemy would have time to shoot them all as dead as doornails.

"I feel sick to my stomach," she said, raising her eyes to Mrs. Johnson's.

"Go outside, my dear. Outside quickly. Don't be sick in here. There's been enough for one day."

"Do you want me to come?" asked Jane.

"No, nobody come," said Edie, getting up slowly and walking out. James was passing the vegetable and looked at her. She tried by stiffening all over to control her blood so that she wouldn't get red.

"Miss Edith has a stomach-ache," said Mrs. Johnson. "Go right ahead, James. The excitement has upset her."

"Edie never gets upset like that," said Jane. "I hope she hasn't got appendicitis."

"Don't invite trouble, child," said Mrs. Johnson.

They all watched Edie as she sat down on the terrace steps waiting, apparently, to be sick.

"She might go a little farther away," said Mrs. Johnson. "James, tell Miss Edith to move out of sight."

"She might need help, Madam," said James, watching Edie over his shoulder, and kept on passing.

Edie looked out to sea and wondered if she were sure, absolutely sure. She had only seen him in glimpses. But, as she thought, she became surer, because she understood what he must have done. Gone into those bushes and then turned out of them behind the stable, gone past the bridge after the sentry had run over when the lieutenant whistled, and then calmly walked back to Mrs. Johnson's along the shell road like any ordinary person when everybody was looking for him in the other direction. That settled it. Still, it didn't settle what to do. Where were those old militias anyway? If she made a dash for the beach, would they still be there and what would James do to her family in the meantime?

It was warm in the sun, and through the smell of Mrs. Johnson's pines came the cool sweet smell of the sea. It would be terrible to be in jail. And she had made a mistake. He was an awfully good-looking man when his hair was brushed. Edie relaxed a little. He looked something like Arsène Lupin in that play Father had taken them to.

The harbor itself was dark blue now and the sky orange. Some people had been lucky enough to be able to get to their boats and there were sails up, flapping and drying. How would you like to go to jail, Mr. Arsène Lupin, and never see all this again? Once more she realized that it would be she who would send him there. That good-looking, awfully brave man. He might be a murderer, though!

Edie got up. She couldn't stand her thoughts any more.

"I'm all right now," she said, as she went back into the dining room.

"Will you have some dessert, Miss?" said James.

She looked right at him casually. "Yes, please."

"Ice cream on top of soup," said Mrs. Johnson. "Well, you had better go right home after dinner."

With those beautiful words it did not take them long to escape as soon as Mrs. Johnson had had her coffee, but Edie found that the curiosity of her family was beyond anything.

"What happened to *you?*"

"Did you see a ghost or something?"

"You looked like a piece of cheese."

"Did Mrs. Johnson get your goat?"

Edie tossed her hair back. "Don't you wish you knew?" she said.

They went to see if the soldier was still at the bridge. He was, but he was another one. They stood far enough off so that he would not think they were trying to cross and asked questions.

"Did you catch the burglar?" called Edie.

"No, ma'am," said this soldier, "not yet."

"That means, I suppose," said Hubert, "that he's right here somewhere. Not a pleasant thought, I must say."

"Be sure and look under your bed, General," said Theodore.

"Just what I was thinking of doing."

She held them all in the hollow of her hand, thought Edie, just the way it said in books. Maybe he *was* a murderer, but she guessed at any rate she wouldn't tell until morning. He would probably murder fat Mrs. Johnson first anyway. She would look under her own bed, and lock her door too, and maybe not leave her window open for just one night, if she could think of a good excuse for Jane. It would be so absolutely terrible to be put in jail.

CHAPTER SIX

The Jewels

No matter how things may have been inside all the Cares during the first two weeks after the hurricane, outside all was "peace profound and heavenly light" as Theodore remarked. Edie, backing away from the goat who had grown quite a good pair of horns during the summer, had stepped in her own elephant trap and put her knee out of joint. The trap should have been filled up by the mess made by the hurricane and it was, but only with pine needles from the branch that had fallen over it. When that was removed, it was practically as good as ever. Everyone agreed that Mr. Parker had been the hero of the occasion. Even though Edie had screamed and beaten him on the head with her fists when he took hold of her leg, he had somehow given it the right jerk to put it back in place and then ordered her, on pain of jerking it again, to stay there without moving until the doctor came. He had played solitaire with her to while away the time, kept Lou from climbing over her to give her kisses, and ordered Gander to bring out her dinner on a tray while she, like a princess, reclined on all the window-seat cushions that could be collected. Luckily the weather had turned and it was as clear as crystal. More luckily still, the others thought, particularly Mr. Parker, the doctor put Edie on crutches, and everybody could have a rest. Theodore did not have to worry about her taking the *P.D.Q.*, while he was playing golf, in order to go out to the wreck of the white yacht and look for Mrs. Johnson's jewels. Hubert didn't have to watch out for fear she would cut the legs off any more of his pants. Jane did not have to keep a lookout that her tennis racquet would be used to keep crabs from getting out of the bait pail, and Mr. Parker could really have a moment's summer vacation because he knew where she was the livelong day. This, for the most part, was in a chair on the anchored float, fishing. The pier was beyond repair and would have to wait until Aunt Louise came home and decided what to do about it, but the float with the help of the part-time man, Mrs. Johnson's chauffeur, two boys from the village, Mr. Parker, and Theodore and Hubert had been gotten into the water and made fast to some gigantic stones and a couple of extra anchors that were found in the barn. It would not weather the slightest storm, but it was good enough to swim and fish from and Edie liked fishing. She had tried, but found it impossible to get much of anywhere at the beach on crutches. On the sand they sank in, and on the shell roads they tipped and slid. She was quite certain that to have that pain in her knee once was enough. All the others had to do was get bait for her every day and eat what she caught.

"Eels, too?" asked The Fair Christine.

"Yup," said Edie.

But Cook refused to have eels in her kitchen, so that was all right, and scup were very good. Once in a while when

Edie caught a tautog, that was even better, and it was divided up in small pieces so it would go around.

"I do believe her greatest hope is to catch a horseshoe crab," said Hubert, "and make us eat that."

He was wrong, though. Edie had a hope bigger than anyone suspected, that she would be well enough to board Shaw Wells's sloop before it was taken away. It was still there right at the side veranda door with the bowsprit still looking as if it would like to get in. Two days after the storm some men had come and built a cradle for it, and later a letter came for Theodore that gave him strict instructions. At least he said so, and after that he slept in it every night and locked it up in the daytime. Shaw Wells had been silly enough to get appendicitis right in the middle of the hurricane, and as it had taken a long time to get to the hospital, he had to stay a long time in bed.

"He doesn't want anyone tampering with the sloop," Theodore reported.

"I don't believe it," Edie had said. "You're just being mean."

"All right," said Theodore, "you can go and get the letter if you like; it's in the right-hand drawer of my bureau. If you make a mess of my ties, I'll carve up Widgy and feed him to the fishes."

When she came back with the letter, he folded it up so that she could see only two lines. "And whatever you do," it said, "keep that young sister of yours out. Mine's nosy enough, but yours takes the cake."

"Satisfied?" said Theodore.

Then she had hurt her knee and could only keep willing,

while she fished, that Shaw Wells's appendix would be worse than her dislocation, as Mr. Parker called it, and that she would get well first and find a way.

There was another thing she had to think about too. Her search for Mrs. Johnson's jewels had been interrupted. If she was not going to tell on James and get him sent to jail, then she distinctly felt she ought to find the jewels. It had not seemed at first a very hard thing to do; she had been so sure they must be right around somewhere—probably scattered through the blue- and bayberry bushes beside the barn where she had seen him disappear, and so she had spent hours with Widgy on her hands and knees crawling through the underbrush. Some days she had been able to persuade Hubert to help, but no man could stand such a thing for long, and he had said pretty soon that he would rather keep his eyes in his head than have them hung on a blueberry bush and what did he care about Mrs. Johnson's jewels.

"Anybody'd think the guy had told you what he did with them," he said through the stems. "Ouch! Will you stop slapping branches in my face?"

"*Excuse me,*" said Edie. "Why don't you hunt in your own place instead of following me?"

"I just want to see you pick an emerald and a string of pearls out of a snake hole," said Hubert. "I wouldn't miss it for the world."

"You mean there are snakes here?"

"Snakes and snails and puppy dogs' tails." He made snarling noises at Widgy, so that he went into barking hysterics. He really wasn't much good.

Also there were ticks, and they got them just like the dogs. They had to detick each other every time before they could go back into the house. Sometimes they had not been thorough enough, and ticks were found on other people. Hood complained that The Fair Christine and Lou were being poisoned.

"Give it up, kid," said Hubert. "I'm weak from loss of blood myself."

She gave up the blue- and bayberry bushes, but she crawled under the barn, examined the mulberry tree for holes, looked in the leaves of the half-grown cabbages in the vegetable garden, and dug up her own fifty-cent piece at the corner of the boathouse. If she had thought that a good place, why shouldn't James if he had had time?

That he'd had hardly any time at all she found out through Lou, who was liable to put anything she liked the look of into her mouth. Edie found her sitting in the canvas swing one morning sucking something so big she had to give it her whole attention.

"What have you got in your mouth, Lou?" Edie had asked. They all had to keep asking her every so often because Hood was quite sure she would never live to grow up, but be choked with a stone.

"Nothing," said Lou.

So Edie had had to extract it, and it turned out to be one of Mrs. Johnson's sapphire rings, which meant, it was easy to see, that it had been dropped because somebody was in such a hurry.

Theodore had thought that after that it would be a cinch.

Lou could simply take them to where she had found it, but he should have known better. Everyone tried to get her to tell them, separately and together, but Lou said she didn't know and kept on saying it and wouldn't take them anywhere.

"You give me back my candy," was all she would say.

"She's mad at you," said Chris. "I can tell."

It had become quite clear to Edie that the jewels could not be very far away. Lou never went anywhere. Edie had planned to search the house from cellar to attic, but she had not had time.

Now, naturally, without anyone on the watch James could come back and get the jewels and take them whenever he felt like it. On his day off he would get rid of them. There were lots of people living in Aunt Louise's, but there were lots of days too when everybody was somewhere else and it would be easy enough for him to grab them from their hiding place and get away. This, of course, was why he was still staying at Mrs. Johnson's. She knew he was there because every now and then she could see him from the float. He would come out as calm as day and shake his duster or just stand admiring the view. She hoped one morning as she was putting a piece of clam on her hook and James had stood on Mrs. Johnson's terrace longer than usual that he was not also wondering whether he could get her as well as the jewels. She didn't think he knew, but he might. After this thought she was glad that her knee kept her where she could be seen by somebody almost all the time. When it began to get better and she could walk a little, she kept herself in sight so persistently that it began to be noticed.

"Goodness gracious, Miss Edith," said Hood on the beach one day, "haven't you anything better to do than disturb these children?"

"I was only showing them how to collect a little seaweed," said Edie.

"And get themselves drownded," said Hood, who thought she would get "drownded" herself if she was in an inch of water.

"Let me do it, let me do it, Mith-thes," said Lou, taking a step into the water.

"That's what she means," said The Fair Christine.

Edie hobbled back to the house and the big window seat. Gander was always moving around there somewhere. She would give up hunting for a while and read every book in Aunt Louise's big chests until she was well. In the meantime, she could keep an eye on the sloop. Maybe Theodore would make one little mistake sometime and forget to lock up, and pretty soon she would be able to climb the cradle.

Aunt Louise had a pretty good collection of books, she found. She had had two children and one of them had died, so she had kept all his books in the chest in the wicker chair room. They were moldering away, but perfectly good after you had wiped them a bit. Edie had rather forgotten Gander and everything else by the time she was in the middle of *Tom Sawyer*. But her eye was attracted by something that moved in the hall. She looked over her book. There was James! He spoke at once.

"You alone, miss?"

"Oh no," said Edie quickly. "Gander," she called, "Ga-a-ander."

"Yes, miss," said Gander's voice, almost under their noses. She was in the dining room polishing wood, and she came in with a rag and the polish can. "Here's Mrs. Johnson's butler," said Edie, fixing her eyes on her book again as if it was nothing at all that James had come in the front part of the house without making a sound. It was something to Gander, though.

"Why aren't you afther ringing the bell, man," she said, putting her hands on her hips, rag, can, and all. "Is it gentry you've gotten to be?"

"Now, Miss O'Hara," said James, smiling pleasantly, "no offense, please. The madam sent me on an errand, and since I found no one in the back premises and knew the other young ladies and gentlemen were out in the boats, I undertook to deliver it to this young lady here."

"And what's your errand, may I ask?"

James did not hesitate a second.

"The madam would like to borrow the Sunday's paper," he said, "if you have it on hand. Ours went out to the bin by mistake."

Gander found it for him on the magazine table and saw him severely out the door. She had no use for butlers at any time. She said they were sheep in wolves' clothing, and she had not stopped grumbling when she came back through the hall.

"Would you credit the *ow*dacity of that one," she said, flicking her rag about. "Walking in as proud as you please without a by-your-leave or a knock on the door."

"Maybe you better lock it," said Edie.

"And a lot of good would that do with yourselves running backwards and forwards the whole day."

She finally said she had put a flea in the ear of his honor and went back to work.

Edie was not able to go back to reading *Tom Sawyer*. In fact, it made her feel terribly uneasy to go on reading it. She was just like Tom, and James was the Indian. She saw perfectly that he had come in hoping they were all out of the way. Her first thought was that she had better tell quickly. Who? Mrs. Johnson wouldn't believe her and she doubted whether Mr. Parker would either. For some strange reason he believed like Ted that Edith had a wonderful imagination. It was very annoying. Maybe she would tell Jane. But Jane had more imagination than anyone and would get as excited as a horse. The thing to do was to find the jewels first because now she could be perfectly sure they were in the house. Why otherwise had James come in? If they were anywhere outside, he could have gone down the shell drive without a person noticing anything wrong about it. All the servants at the beach went for walks—you might meet a maid or two anywhere. But they didn't come into people's houses without knocking, no sir.

The very next day Edie was liberated by the doctor. He put a rubber bandage on her knee and said: "All right, young lady, but favor it, favor it." Her behavior after this puzzled the others. She seemed to be favoring it more than was necessary. It was hard even to get her to go swimming.

They talked her over on the float after she had said she didn't want to swim today.

"So doesn't a fish," Hubert had said rudely, but she just answered that she was favoring her knee.

"Maybe she's going to turn into a permanent invalid," he said on the float, forgetting his own decline, "and live in a darkened room. I hope she won't expect us to read to her on her bed of pain."

"I hope she doesn't do it till Madam gets home," said Jane.

"Nonsense," said Theodore, giving the water a push with his foot. "She's just simmering. In a couple of days she'll go off like a firecracker. I've seen it happen before." He took a dive after a clam shell that he had thrown in ahead of him, and when he came up, tossed it to Mr. Parker. "Don't look so bleak, old man. It's not our little sister who'll get the explosion in the face. It'll be us. It always is."

Mr. Parker dived after the clam shell, but not as if he had any pleasure in it, and it got away from him. "I wonder what she's doing now," he said after he had pulled himself up on the float.

He would have been surprised but not alarmed at what Edie was doing unless he might have imagined she was the thief herself. As soon as she saw them all safely down by the water, she began examining every nook and cranny in the downstairs part of the house. It got her nowhere and she had to spring back to the couch as she heard them coming. At least she knew the jewels were not on the first floor.

"Will you kindly tell me what you were doing in my room last night," said Theodore the next day. "Oh yes, I saw you from the *Q,* so don't deny it, but I couldn't see what you were up to."

"I was just practicing walking," said Edie.

Hubert and Jane found her practicing walking in odd places and at odd hours too.

"Why not try it outdoors," said Hubert. "There's a lot more room."

"It's rougher," said Edie.

She ransacked Mr. Parker's room when he and the others had all gone for the mail together.

"What are you going to do while we're gone?" Mr. Parker had asked, looking at her hard.

"Nothing," said Edie. "Why?"

Whatever his suspicions, he found her in the same spot on the hall floor making Widgy find his way out of the butterfly net, when he got back. He had no thought-reading machine, so he could not know that she had found nothing in his room either. She was so completely discouraged that she accepted Jane's invitation that afternoon to rewind the rolls of the player piano.

"Maybe," said Jane, "Aunt Louise likes the old thing so much she might have it fixed."

The way they did it was for Edie to stand out on the balcony holding one end of the paper while Jane came toward her from the boathouse door rolling as tight as she could. It was quite a success, and after they had done six or seven rolls, Edie wanted to try one.

"It's had two weeks to dry," she said. "It might go without fixing."

It went as if it had asthma, choking in places and wheez-

ing in others. The music came out as it should, but
the piano's insides complained loudly through it.

"I can't stand it," said Jane, putting her fingers in her
ears. "It sounds like torture to me."

"Go away, then," said Edie. "You can't torture things that
aren't alive. Go away. I'm going to make Widgy sing. It's
just the kind of noises he likes to do it for."

Now she knew where to look! In the boathouse of course,
and probably in the piano. It sounded exactly as if diamonds
and pearls wrapped round its insides were giving it spasms.
But she had a hard time getting rid of Jane who thought
her playing would tear it to pieces.

"It won't either," said Edie. "It'll just warm it up like a
good canter. Come on, Widge. Yow, yow, yow. Begin, you
dumb dog."

Widgy and the piano did the trick. Edie waited until Jane
should have had time to get back to the house, keeping Widgy going with the loud pedal and her own accom-
paniment. Then she let the piano groan to a stop and started
her investigation full of hope and excitement. It was true
that James might have come and got them during the night,
but then, he might not; as long as someone remembered it,
the boathouse was locked at night, and besides Theodore
was not so far away, asleep in Shaw Wells's sloop.

Edie very nearly spoiled all her plans by getting stuck
in the player piano. Its works were so far down that she had
to go in head first through the top and leave her legs kicking, and, once in, there seemed no way to get out and no
noise to make that would bring any help. Jane, she knew,
would think—and tell them—it was more and worse

Widgy. She was there long enough to remember Mr. Lumsden and his rush of blood to the head and to make a short prayer that she would not get *that*. She also prayed that no one would find her in this position, and both her prayers were answered. She managed to find a thin ledge with her groping hands and to push herself up enough to get one arm into freedom, but the experience had shaken her. She sat on the piano stool disconsolately. If the jewels were in there, they would have to stay until she could get a searchlight or some matches and, feeling it tenderly, she was sure that waving it in the air hadn't done her knee any good either. She limped half-heartedly here and there looking without much hope in the pockets of the billiard table and in the drawer where the mouse nest had been. No more mice, poor things. Only some seaweed with shells in it washed in by the hurricane. She stood at the balcony door looking the room over as if she might see jewels hung up on the walls. Not a sapphire or ruby was to be seen unless that thing that glinted behind the boathouse door was one. She hurried over. It might at least be a ring! It wasn't of course. It was a key. It probably belonged to something of Cousin Blade's, put there ages ago and forgotten. It was a padlock key, and there weren't any padlocks around that she could remember. And then she did remember where she had seen one. On the afterhatch of Shaw Wells's sloop. Ha, ha, so this was where Theodore kept the key, and he came and got it every night just before going to bed.

"Widgy, we've got it," said Edie to his panting face. "Do you know that, dumb dog? We've got the key to the sloop.

Only you can't come. You'll have to stay here awhile. I'll be back in two shakes."

The first thing to do was to see what everyone else was doing. It seemed bad luck to find three of them in the chintz parlor eating so big a tea they would never be through.

"We were just going to get you," said Jane.

"Thanks," said Edie. "You might have come before you ate all the sandwiches."

"We weren't coming to get you for tea," said Hubert. "Prima donnas are always too fat anyhow. We've all been invited to a picnic on the outer beach by the Harlows. Do you want to come?"

"No, thanks very much," said Edie, feeling the key in her pocket. "Do I have to?"

"Well, if you don't Si thinks he better stay at home with you."

"Oh no! Why?"

"If I could dream," said Mr. Parker, "that you'd keep out of trouble—"

"Mr. Parker," said Edie very seriously, "if I make you a solemn promise I won't leave this place, will you go?"

Hubert sat back and put his hands behind his head.

"Don't do it, Si; she's too anxious to get rid of you."

"How about it, Mr. Parker," said Edie. "I'd feel very badly if I spoiled your fun, and I won't go further than the end of the lawn. Shake on it!" She got up and offered her hand.

"You better add not on the roof either, or up a chimney, or down a well," said Hubert.

"Yes?" said Mr. Parker to Edie.

"Yes," said Edie. "Anyhow there aren't any wells."

They shook hands and Edie ate all that was left of the tea cakes, which in the end she considered was a very wise thing to have done. One thing, however, was not yet settled.

"Where's Ted?" she asked, as they got up to get ready. "Isn't he going?"

"Mrs. Palmer's got him again," said Jane. "And he won't be home for ages probably. She takes him swimming after they play golf."

"Well, I won't bother him," said Edie righteously. "I'm going on with Widgy's singing lessons. *In the house,*" she said, looking at Mr. Parker.

"Quick," said Hubert, "let us fly."

Edie watched them safely away from the shore and rowing across the harbor. She blew a kiss to them from the dining-room window, not so they could see, naturally, otherwise they would be back to see what was the matter, and then she hobbled as fast as she could to the ladder that leaned against the sloop. Once in the cabin she thought it only a good precaution to shut the doors and pull the hatch to. If anyone went by, they would probably not notice that the padlock was not in its hole. As another slight precaution she had hung it back on the brass latch. She wanted to take her time. This was the kind of boat she herself wished with all her heart that she could have, and she was going to look at every part of it.

When she had examined the bunks and lain down on them, the racks above them and what was in them, the little toilet, and the miniature curtains that pulled across the portholes, Edie moved quietly and reverently into the galley. Nothing had disappointed her. Everything was better than she had expected it would be. She might not love Shaw Wells since he had refused to lend her an oar, but he knew a good kind of boat, and in spite of having been through a hurricane, it was as clean as a hundred whistles. She could not help running her hand along the polished wood and touching at least once everything she saw.

The galley was small, smaller than she would have thought a place to cook in could be. You would have had to shave Cook down on all sides to get her in at all. There was just room for a stove with a rack around it, in case of bad weather, and a chest opposite you could sit on—it was probably full of provisions. Yup. She opened the cover and saw a bag of flour and boxes of hardtack. There were cupboards wherever there could be a cupboard, and all of them were lined with things to eat. Mostly baked beans, baked beans, baked beans. She thought Theodore had said how good the food was on Shaw Wells's boat. He had probably made it up because he had been cook. If she ever had a sloop, she would line it with flagiolette beans, cranberry sauce, and fish chowder.

Beyond the galley was an open space with a ladder that led up to the forward hatch. That, she could see, was locked on the inside with a fat brass hook that fitted into a fat eye. On either side were recesses where the sails were kept and two long water tanks. She sighed. It had everything. If she had had a boat like this, she could have stayed at Millard's Cove for a lifetime. As she backed into the galley again, she lifted up the small kettle to admire it. It was so perfectly round and squatty, it would sit through any storm. And heavy too, no doubt with an extra bottom, like extra lead on a boat's keel. She still had it in her hand and was going to take off the cover when through her interest she gradually heard voices—men's voices, Theodore's voice. Drat! Now she was in a fix. Mrs. Palmer must have let him off early and he had come home to dinner. Well, she was not going to come out to be called names in front of everybody he had brought with him. She would wait till they went into the house. She put the kettle with infinite care back on the stove, but it was so heavy it made a tiny clunk just the same. Nothing happened, so she sat down on the chest opposite holding her breath. What was Ted bringing a lot of men home for anyway? She bet Cook didn't have enough to eat for a crowd; anyhow, her nerves were still bothering her, she said, and she would only be expecting Theodore.

Edie waited to hear the veranda door slam. Instead she heard a man quite close to the boat say: "We can work till dark, if that's agreeable to you." And another man said: "Get out them rollers, Jim. It won't take so long at that. She's trick and trim enough and it's downhill all the way."

Edie blew out her breath until she was entirely empty. Theodore had not been with Mrs. Palmer at all; he had been at the boat yard persuading the men to get Shaw Wells's sloop into the water after regular working hours. He had been saying for days that it had been on the lawn long enough, but he had not been able to get anyone to come because they had been too busy repairing their own damage. She was caught this time. Still, she would wait.

They might not come into the cabin and after the sloop was in the water she could swim ashore. Shaw Wells's mooring was not so awfully far out in the harbor and it would be low tide.

For a long time Edie was kept in the galley while she felt and tried to figure out the movements of the sloop. Now they were lifting the cradle with the block and tackle; now they let it down on the rollers; now it began to move away from the front door, she was sure. The wait then was so long and it was so still that she thought she might risk an escape, but she looked cautiously out a porthole first. She could tell that she had reached the boathouse and that now they would have to turn to go down the ravine. They must have gone off to get something to clean out the blueberry bushes. She took a careful step toward the hatch. Heavens no! There were all their voices again telling each other to "take it easy," "make it taut."

"Don't let her get away from you, whatever you do," she heard Theodore say anxiously.

She sat down again on the chest. The little kettle was all she had to look at, so she considered it with her chin in her hand. It was a cute kettle all right, but she would like to know how they made it so heavy. From here she couldn't see any extra bottom, and if that was inside, there would hardly be room for water. It was so near she hardly needed to lean forward to get it by the handle and lift it onto her lap. Very noiselessly and slowly she took off the lid. Bother! It was too dark in here to see a thing. She put in her hand and pulled it right out again. Rocks! Somebody had filled it with sharp rocks. That was a joke on Shaw

Wells. Or had he put them in himself to keep the kettle steady? Because she had nothing better to do, her fist closed on a handful and brought them out. In the dim light she thought they were queer-looking things. They had strings on them and they were not gray or black, they were— Edie's heart almost stopped. They had white strings on them and they glinted. With her left hand she steadily and quietly put the kettle back on the stove. She took her right hand just as it was, dripping with something, into the cabin and held it up to a porthole.

It was fat Mrs. Johnson's jewelry all right. The white strings were the pearls, it was a diamond bracelet that glinted, and her fist was full of rings. Her first thought was to pop out the hatchway with the jewels in her hands and show them to Theodore, and she might have done it except that the sloop began to move just then and tip forward, so that she sat down hard against the foot of the bunk. The men must be doing the ticklish job of sliding her down the ravine hill. She better leave them alone till they got her to the shore. It wouldn't take long.

By the time she could hear water, Edie had had another and better idea. *She* would take the jewels back to fat Mrs. Johnson herself. She had had all the trouble and done all the work and had James come in and look at her from the hall. Her insides laughed as she thought of Theodore's sleeping every night with them nearly on top of his nose. He wasn't going to get them now and spoil everything with one of his fierce scoldings. She leaned back on the bunk cushions to enjoy the last part of the trip. The boat was on an even keel now and the worst was over. All they would have to do was roll the cradle into the water and float her off—a lucky thing because it was nearly dark. She heard Theodore pointing out the right mooring and realized that the men from the boat yard meant to tow her out and tie her up. Gander must have come out and fussed at him to come in and eat. What luck! She wouldn't have to be afraid of *him* any more.

The last part of the trip was a pleasure and so was listening to the boat yard men row away talking to each other in the dusk. Edie took the kettle off the stove, opened the afterhatch, and sat enjoying the evening air a hundred yards or so out in the harbor while she considered how many clothes to take off for her swim ashore. As she began to think of it, she had a nasty doubt. That kettle was heavy. She hefted it once more. It wasn't so much its heaviness, but how could she swim with that kind of thing attached to one hand? It would be like trying to drag an anchor. She hung her head, seeing her beautiful triumph go up in smoke because there was one thing she was not going to do, and that was let Mrs. Johnson's jewels sink to the bottom of the harbor after she had had the luck to find them. If she could only take them without the kettle. Why not, she thought, sitting up again. She could wear them like Mrs. Johnson herself. Slowly and experimentally, after taking off her dress, she took the jewels out. The bracelets she fastened on her ankles, the rings she put on her thumbs and the pearls around her waist, knotting them up because they were so long. Three or four chains she wound around her wrists and some pins she stuck through a reef knot she had seen in the bunk rack. This she tied around her neck. When she stood up, it was a shock to be pulled at by such a lot of things, but she made herself think it wasn't really so bad and anyway she was sure she could do it. There was still some waiting to do; she could still be seen from the shore. She would relax on the hatchway steps to be rested for her last great endeavor. While she waited, she put up her nose to catch that wonderful perfume of the sea and shore, and she listened to the utter, utter stillness. Everyone must be in their houses after dinner. I'm starved, she thought. It was just about time to go, and yet she hardly wanted to get under way.

Into the stillness, like a bird chuckling, came the sound of oars. Edie almost felt her ears stand up like a dog's. Yes! It was, and getting nearer quickly. She could hear them squeak against the oarlocks. She pushed herself up to look and saw a blacker shape on the water and, besides that, some phosphorescence. She could not see who it was, but she realized it was a good rower; he made almost no noise and came on steadily. James! Mrs. Johnson's finished dinner and he's gotten away. He had seen the boat being put out, of course, and had come to get the jewels. I'm a goner, thought Edie. If the jewels had only still been in the kettle, she might have saved herself at least, but they were all over her. She could never get them off in time, and he would certainly tear her apart to get them. Her panic almost made her jump into the water there and then, but she saw that by turning the boat a little he could catch her and, if he wanted, hit her with an oar. She slid into the cabin, closed the hatch, and then, groping through the galley, got to the forward ladder. There she undid the hook that held the

doors together and opened them a slit so that she could
hear. The rower was near by this time. He would certainly
come in by the cockpit, though, and while he was tying up
the rowboat, she could crawl out and let herself into the
water. If she could do it silently enough, she could get a
good head start.

Edie waited, hardly able to breathe. Gee, I mustn't be
like this in the water she warned herself. She heard James
ship his oars and get aboard, and she waited even then;
when he got to the cabin, she would go. With great care
she pulled the doors back and got through on her hands
and knees, having to move with dreadful slowness on account of the rings and chains. Even then, they nicked the
deck and made small sounds. She went into the water with
a soft slop, but it wasn't much; it wouldn't have been anything if one of the chains had not struck a cleat and made
a chink. Perhaps he hadn't heard, as he was moving round
himself. She set off anyhow as fast as she could, swimming
breast stroke to make less noise. In fact, she found it impossible to swim any other way because her arms and legs
were so loaded with bangles.

Whether he had heard or not, *she* could hear that James
was on deck and she had to wonder, as she breathed long
breaths and pushed herself steadily forward like an old tug,
how much he could see. She had not expected him to dare
to use a light, and when it shone behind her, she was ap-
palled, until with a hurried look she saw that he was pointing it toward the harbor side. He was not sure where the
sounds were coming from—that was it. Then she heard
his quick steps toward the bow and the light shone in her

direction. She did not think it reached her, but her swimming was not so quiet now; she was getting tired and had begun to splash. The light went off, there was some sound, maybe swearing, and then the noises became quite plain. He was yanking the boat in and then fitting the oars in the oarlocks entirely recklessly just as he had used the light. He must be desperate, and she would have to go faster. She thrashed and splashed with the jewels clogging her every stroke, but she made more headway. I'm dying, she thought, I'm almost dead, and then like paradise, as James came on with deadly long pulls of the oars, her feet touched bottom. Getting out of the water was like being in a nightmare. If he shone his lights now, he could see her easily and shoot her with no trouble at all while her feet were stuck in the sand, but he didn't stop for that. He was evidently quite sure he was going to catch her, so much so that by the time she was at the top of the beach and his boat grounded, he stopped to pull it up out of the way of the tide. Edie thought even as she ducked into the black path that it was a stupid thing to do. Why should he care about Mrs. Johnson's boat? Perhaps he meant to take the jewels out to sea because he was going to get them after all. The path was all uphill, and though the bushes had been partly cleared when the sloop came down, she hadn't any more breath and her knee wouldn't hold her. She was having to help herself along with her hands.

She did have enough head start, however, to get to the top of the ravine and crawl out onto the lawn, where the lights from Aunt Louise's shone clear to the boathouse. There she stayed on her hands and knees with her head down, fixed and finished, and James, on the run, tripped over her and fell flat on his face with the wind knocked out of him. When he grunted, Edie looked up.

"Theodore!" she said. "It's *you!*"

"It's you, you mean," said Theodore jerkily. He held his ribs rolling from side to side. "I thought you were the burglar. But I might have known it, I might have known it."

Edie's relief was so enormous that for once in her life, just this once, she began to cry, tremendous sobs that shook her back and forth.

"Hey," said Theodore, "is there something the matter with *you?*"

"I thought you were going to kill me."

"Who—*me?*"

"No—James."

"Who!" said Theodore, sitting up.

"James," said Edie, trying to sit up too in order to wipe her face.

"Are you really a lunatic," asked Theodore earnestly, "or are you just pretending to be? And will you kindly tell me what you were doing—" Then he saw that she was half dressed and covered with some sort of ornaments and became speechless. As he told Hubert that night, he thought they would be taking their sister to an asylum in the morning.

"Oh," said Edie, embarrassed by his staring. "They're fat Mrs. Johnson's and I had to take off my dress to swim."

Theodore lay back again on the grass to try to make head or tail of it.

"You know," he said finally, seriously, "there's such a

thing as going too far. People might get the idea you *were* balmy."

"All right," said Edie, "we'll go to Mrs. Johnson's right now."

"Not like that, you won't," said Theodore quickly, getting up to stop her.

She could not have done it anyway as she even needed Ted's help to get to her feet. Very graciously he allowed her to lean on his arm as if she were a lady, but he would not let her go into Aunt Louise's without being decently clothed.

"They're all in there," he explained. "Si Parker and the Harlows too. Si thought you would be in trouble and sure enough—"

"Oh," said Edie, stricken, "I promised I wouldn't go off the lawn."

"And why did you?" asked Theodore with the utmost politeness.

"I was taken in the sloop," said Edie.

It was all beyond his weak brain to understand, Ted said, but he would grant Edie this. When she wanted to, she could make things as clear as mud.

"You'll see," said Edie.

She had to stand on one leg in the shadows while he went in to get something to cover her nakedness. He was so proper he couldn't even stand the sight of a petticoat.

"They've vamoosed," he told her when he came back. "They've probably gone to watch Si hang himself. Here, put this on anyway; it's all I could find."

It was her Sunday coat, of course, and there would be a

good deal of salt water on it in a few minutes, but Edie could not wait. As she limped down the shell road, she tried to explain.

"I suppose you know there's a reward," said Ted when he could see through a glass darkly. "One thousand bucks," he added solemnly.

"It won't do me any good," said Edie, "you know that. Father'll just put it in the bank."

"Well, what would *you* do with a thousand bucks?"

"Buy a boat," said Edie promptly.

"You ought to have a medal at any rate," said Theodore generously, "for bravery I should think."

"Well, thanks," said Edie, feeling bashful.

"But if you do get a boat, I hope you'll remember I guarded those things every night for two weeks."

"Well, sure," said Edie, very much wishing to be generous too.

Mrs. Johnson's house was lighted from cellar to attic as if she were having a party, but she wasn't. She had just kept it that way, she said, ever since the jewels were taken. James, of course, locked up for the night later on. They knew enough not to go to the front door where he might open it for them. Instead they walked through the pines and up the terrace steps to the big glass doors. Mrs. Johnson was sitting inside by herself looking at the newspaper, and it did not make a good impression on her when they scratched at the door.

"Hmm," she said, "rather late for a call isn't it, but come in for a minute, I suppose. Will you sit down?"

"No," said Edie. "Look!" And she took off her coat.

Mrs. Johnson herself sat down so that she jolted, and at once for no good reason became very angry.

"Did you steal my jewels, you naughty child? I've had my suspicions ever since that episode with your sister. Sucking sapphires indeed! It's a wonder she isn't dead!"

"That's just what Hood says," said Edie, trying to be agreeable.

"And why haven't you any clothes on!" said Mrs. Johnson with sudden surprise and disapproval.

Both Edie and Theodore attempted to explain this at the same time, and in the end they did not think they had been very successful, Edie wanted to tell so much, and Theodore so little. The one thing that Mrs. Johnson did get was that James was a burglar.

"My new wonderful James!" said Mrs. Johnson, sitting back. "Impossible!" Edie had known it was going to happen and was ready for it. All she wanted to do was get rid of the jewels. "Here," she said, "take them off," and she held out her wrists and wiggled her thumbs to get the rings to fall off into what there was of Mrs. Johnson's lap.

"Ring for James!" said Mrs. Johnson, clutching the rings but not looking at them. "There's the bell, boy; do as I say. We'll fix these accusations immediately. They say you have quite an imagination, Miss Edith Cares."

"Help me take 'em off just the same," said Edie, unwinding the pearls and trying to undo the string at her neck as if she had become frightened of them.

"If James is coming, hadn't she better put her coat on?" said Theodore

"This is no time to be prudish," said Mrs. Johnson. "Yes, Marie? What's the matter with you? Have you seen a ghost?"

The maid was standing at the door, trembling all over.

"I don't know how to tell you, Madam," she said. "But James has left the house, and the flat silver's gone with him, Madam."

Whereupon, Theodore told Hubert that night after they had closed their door on the world of females, the maid threw her apron over her head and went off to the kitchen, caterwauling.

Mrs. Johnson caterwauled too for a moment, at least she screamed, and said to send for the police. "Instantly," she said. "Instantly!"

But since the militia had left nearly ten days ago, there was only Captain Harbuck and he had gone to his cousin's funeral in East Barnet, the operator told Theodore, and wouldn't be back until tomorrow night.

"So I had to take the situation in hand," Theodore told Hubert.

He and Edie had picked up the diamonds and pearls that had rolled off Mrs. Johnson's lap and piled them on one of the chair cushions. He made her count them to see if they were all there, and when she said she thought they were, "except the one your sister chewed," she had the nerve to add, he commanded Edie to put on her coat and come home.

"And would you believe it, old man," said Theodore, "she wouldn't stir a stump."

Edie had behaved in the most shameful manner. Even

after Mrs. Johnson had assured her that she would attend to the reward in the morning, she still wouldn't move.

"It's my leg," she said. "It won't hold me up."

And right then and there she had turned green and fallen on the floor.

"Take her home, take her home," said Mrs. Johnson. "What is she fainting for right in my living room!"

"Which," said Theodore, "I had been wanting to do right along." But he had to carry her, and she had not had time to put on her coat, so it had been quite embarrassing when they met Si Parker at Aunt Louise's door and Edie had begun to come to. "Nothing could embarrass that kid, though," said Theodore.

"Let me down," Edie had said. "What are you hugging me for? I just need something to eat." She had looked sideways at Mr. Parker. "I thought you'd gone to hang yourself," she said. "But it wasn't my fault."

"Maybe I'll still do it," said Mr. Parker, "but I think your family's coming home."

"On account of *me?*" said Edie. "Oh, they don't need to do that at all."

"I'd like to think it was on account of me," said poor old Si Parker.

The next day it was bed rest for Edie, at any rate until the doctor could get there, but why should she care? Gander brought up her breakfast tray herself instead of standing at the bottom of the stairs and shrieking for Jane. And on it was an envelope from Mrs. Johnson with a thin piece of paper—"Pay to order of Edith Cares," it said, "$1,000."

Everyone had to see it. Cook came and looked at her from the door and said: "Ye done fine, Miss Edith, keeping us all from being murdered in our beds." Mr. Parker came right in and told her that all was forgiven—he had now heard the whole story, he said—but not forgotten. He hoped he would *never* forget it. Good news kept pouring in. Jane reported that she was sure the mouse mother was alive; she thought she had seen her going toward the boathouse when she was on her way to feed Laza and Jocko. Hubert actually brought her a bunch of flowers and made a low bow as he handed them to her, saying: "For more than exceptional bravery beyond the call of duty!" Theodore, after contemplating the check for a good while, had said: "It won't buy a boat, you know," and had then offered to go partners if he could scrape up a bit more to put with what he had in the savings bank. But what was the best, the very best—no one seemed able to stay away from her room for very long. They kept coming and going and talking and telling over and over. They were all either walking up and down or sitting around when Gander came upstairs a second time, looking, said Hubert, as if she had caught the fainting disease herself.

"Master Theodore," she said through the door, "will you come out here a minute, sir?"

Gander only put on her best manners when something important had happened.

"How do they get the news before anybody else?" said Hubert. "I bet there's something more up."

Theodore was gone quite a while, and the others were just going to follow him when he came back.

"Now keep your shirts on," he said.

"Not unless you tell us," said Edie.

"They've just found a man's body by the railroad tracks," said Theodore. "They think he tried to board the up train in the night and got his neck broken when he fell. And *who* do you think it is?" he said directly to Edie.

"Who?" said Edie.

"Fat Mrs. Johnson's butler. That guy James."

"Oh," said Edie. She looked at her feet. "Oh dear, he was a very good-looking man.

"At least," she said, "he won't have to go to jail."

Looking at her feet and the end of the bed had made her think of something far, far more important.

"Widgy!" she said. "Oh, my poor little dog. Would you get him? He's been shut in the boathouse all night."

"And tell him right away," she called as Jane left immediately, "I'll never, never, never, do it again."

CHAPTER SEVEN

Lou

It was true what Mr. Parker had said. Father and Madam were coming home, but his hopeful expectations of having an easier time when they arrived were not fulfilled. He had to go away himself a week before they came in order to get ready for some more education and, instead, Mr. Carpenter, Father's college friend, sailed down from Bay's Landing with Penelope, his calico cat, to be with them until their honored parent should return. It was a lovely week. They were used to Mr. Carpenter's having good ideas, as he had stayed with them before, but this time they were the best he had ever had. At least Edie thought so.

The first was about mice. Aunt Louise's house was infested with them, Mr. Carpenter said, and for friendship's sake he meant to clean them out.

"With Penelope?" asked Edie while she was being allowed to clean brass on his catboat.

"Not at all," said Mr. Carpenter. "She's far too much of a cat for mice as unsophisticated as yours appear to be." He sent Hubert and Edie in the Ford all up and down the beach villages looking for merciful traps. When they couldn't find any, he changed his plan. "If a cat can watch a mouse hole, so can we," he said. Edie, in the wicker chair room, was set for hours to grab the mouse he had seen go under the wainscoting. She never got one, but Mr. Carpenter did from where he was watching in the hall, and he brought it in to show her. Its little bright eyes and pricked ears stuck up out of the circle of his hand.

"What are you going to do with him?" Edie asked.

"I suppose we might as well let him go," said Mr. Carpenter. "One really isn't enough to make much difference, and he would probably like to get home."

Of all the men she knew—but two, Edie thought, remembering her gold football—she approved of Mr. Carpenter the most.

The next day he asked her if she would like to get something to celebrate the travelers' return.

"What?" said Edie over the top of *Frowzle the Runaway*, which she was reading on the window seat. "If you mean clothes, no."

"Food," said Mr. Carpenter, pushing his lips between his red beard and mustache. "Fooood. Have you ever been lobstering?"

They chugged about the bay in Mr. Carpenter's catboat with Penelope sitting on the hatch, caught up buoys with the boat hook, and then hauled in the pots. It was better than finding Mrs. Johnson's jewels. You never knew what you might get or what Mr. Carpenter would do about it. He had a grudge against starfish.

"Low life," he said. "They eat with their stomachs." And he left them to suffer on the deck. Sculpins and spider crabs he snarled at and threw as far as he could out to sea. Puffers he scratched until they blew up and then whacked to make them pop. When he had taken out the lobsters and the pot was ready to go back in the water, he told Edie to wait a jiffy and he took a small white bag out of his pocket and filled it with silver money, drew its string tight, and tied it to the buoy rope.

"There," he said, flinging the buoy and its cargo over the side, "I pay as I go."

"I thought they were your pots," said Edie.

"Dear me, no," said Mr. Carpenter. "They belong to Sam Portagee, but I know him and he knows me, and between us both we allus agree. Didn't know I could make poetry, didja? We've enough now. You take the helm and head for home."

It crossed Edie's mind more than once that it might almost be more fun living with Mr. Carpenter than with her own family especially on his catboat.

For the evenings Mr. Carpenter had brought fire balloons. They were to while away the time after the work of the busy world was done, he said, which is what they certainly did. So much so that Jane went off to sulk in the boathouse with the player piano, saying she could not stand such stupid people and Theodore, Hubert, and Edie never wanted to go to bed at all.

Fire balloons came out of a flat box neatly pressed together, but when one was shaken out, it became a large real balloon with a small basket held by wires. What made Jane have a fit was that Mr. Carpenter put a big fat lighted candle in the basket while Theodore held the top of the balloon, waited until the heated air made it swell and tug at Theodore's hand, and then said: "Whoosh! Let 'er go." And the balloon did go, sailing off into the night.

"With this fine seaward breeze, my dears, it's as safe as kittens," Mr. Carpenter had said, but still Jane would not stay to enjoy the fun.

When one balloon sailed right for the Harlows' across the harbor, they all raced over there at high speed in the Ford to let them know it was coming, and the Harlows all came out on the lawn to watch it skim over their trees and go out to sea. It made them want fire balloons themselves after Mr. Carpenter had explained that the candle would only stay lighted if the balloon was high in the air. If it came down, it would go out.

"Just so," said Mr. Harlow, who was a scientist. Mrs. Harlow missed it because she was visiting her sister.

The fire balloons lasted right up until the night before Father and Madam arrived. It was really a lovely, lovely week, but they *were* coming and expected to be met at the five o'clock train at the Mount Harbor station by all their family, and two cars, and anyone else, Father said over the telephone, who felt strong enough to help them disembark.

"I don't think he can mean me," said Mr. Carpenter. "I'm a very weak sister when it comes to carrying bags because my beard gets in the way. Hang out the ensign and I'll come back later. Penelope needs recreation."

They had to say good-by to him after lunch and watch him go off in his catboat after bringing up a basket of lobsters and delivering it to Cook.

So it was Theodore who gave the orders about what they

were to do. He and Hubert would drive the cars, he said, and anyone who wanted could have a ride downtown, but they would have to come back on "shanks' mare." The luggage when their parents had gone away, if they would take the trouble to remember, had filled both cars to the brim.

"So just let your minds dwell on what it will be like now," he said.

Especially, they all knew, if Madam had bought any new hats.

Jane and Hubert agreed it would be a pleasure to walk if there was any chance of bags being put on top of them, Edie knew she would get a ride on account of her knee, and Hood when told said that she would see that the children went and came in the goat cart.

"A piece of unexpected nobility, I must say," said Hubert, flicking his napkin across the table at Lou, because to make the goat go at all someone had to hold a bunch of carrots in front of his nose as well as hang on to the bridle. He was fairly big by this time, but had only had training when they had had nothing much else to do.

"It's because she can dress them up and they look so cute holding the reins everyone stops to speak to them," said Jane. "Leave Lou alone, can't you?"

"Ten to one people are stopping to think how silly they look," said Theodore. He did object to being the brother— even the half-brother—of sisters who out of the purest vanity made a display of themselves.

Still, it seemed the only way to solve the problem and, anyway, Hood had made up her mind to it and there was not much to be done after that. She probably knew that if

Lou's legs got tired she would lie down on the road and pretend it was her own little bed. Even leading a goat would be better than that. Afterwards they supposed that Hood had had a premonition and their opinion of her went up by leaps and bounds.

"She must have known how the kid was going to act," Theodore said.

When Madam got off the train in the largest hat she had ever had and a feather boa skirling and flying in the beach breeze, Lou did not know her at all. She stepped up to Edie from the back and said in her loudest voice:

"Mith-thes, who ith that big woman?"

"Shh," said Edie, "it's your mother."

"It ith *not*," said Lou, and she went back to the goat cart, got in, and tried to start up the goat by slapping the reins. Hood had to hold him with both hands.

No amount of persuasion from any of them did any good, and when Madam, after saying "Hello, everybody," and kissing them all as she always did, took a few steps toward her, calling: "My Lou-li," she scrambled from the front seat into the back and crouched there sucking her thumb and rolling her eyes. Father barked, "Louise!" at her, but she rolled her eyes at him too and did not move. With everyone on the station platform looking, it was so awful that even Edie's short hair was not noticed.

"Maybe it's your hat," said Hubert quickly.

"She hasn't much sense some of the time," said Edie.

"You do look awfully young," Jane said.

Theodore thought of mentioning the feather boa, but realized it wasn't very polite and stopped. It must be pretty bad not to be known by your own child and that was a fact, but the worst of it was they all understood what Lou meant. Madam had come back from Paris looking so much like a lady that if you were as young as Lou, how could you tell it was your mother? Saying the right thing seemed impossible.

"She probably thinks you're an ogre," said The Fair Christine.

Well, anyhow, that wasn't it. They stood around awkwardly, hating to see Madam looking as if someone had made her take medicine and Father helplessly pulling his mustache. Good old Hood saved them.

"I'd better take the child home, ma'am. She's not herself," she said, and she turned the goat and started off. Only Lou had time to take out her thumb and say: "Yeth, I am too. Who're you?" and put it in again.

Madam laughed at that and so did Father, so that they all could laugh and then Father took charge. The trunks could be brought to the house this time by the station express wagon. Each of them was to put some one of the smaller bags in the Ford, leaving just room for Hubert and McLean, Madam's maid, and everyone else could pack into the Packard. The Fair Christine could sit on her mother's knee. On the way back they passed the goat cart and covered its passenger with dust as she deserved, but she only stared at them over the top of her thumb.

That was the way she came to supper too, which was dinner tonight on account of Father and Madam, with Mr. Carpenter's lobsters, corn on the cob, and baked Alaska for dessert to make a celebration. Cook and Gander had been at the door.

"Lord love you, your honors," said Cook. "It's a mercy to see this day."

Gander just took coats and gloves and hats as fast as she could saying: "Welcome now, welcome." And then they both went back to finish preparing the feast—with something special too for the children—which Lou could only look at sadly while Chris and the others ate it up.

It took longer than usual in spite of its being so good on account of there being quite a few things that had happened during the summer that it was possible to tell even to Father. Not about Theodore and Mrs. Palmer, naturally, or Edie and Miss Black, or Hubert and Lady Alicia Throg in the wheelbarrow or somehow Mr. Carpenter and the fire balloons, but things got started with Edie's hair. She had to get up and stand backwards to show it off.

"Shocking," said Father.

They went on hurriedly to the hurricane.

"Did you know we had one?" asked Jane.

Everyone had to talk then no matter how full their mouths were of lobster.

"Do you know what Jane and Theodore did?" said Edie. She told about the swim in from the *P.D.Q.*

"Do you know what *Edith* did?" asked Theodore in revenge.

"Caught a burglar," said The Fair Christine before anyone else. But the rest of them could talk faster and told the story.

"Jane won the tennis tournament incidentally," said Hubert.

"And Chris knows how to swim now."

"Hubert had a cruise on a yacht."

"He knows a Viz-count and a Viz-countess," said Edie.

"Wait, wait, wait," said Father. "Go a little slower, please. Correct her somebody." He put both hands over his ears. When he took them down, he said: "And Louise, if you don't eat your dinner, you had better go upstairs."

Lou crouched down lower and didn't move.

It seemed a pity that Father had to notice that silly Lou. It was all because Madam kept looking at her, they supposed. Jane drew a long breath.

"And do you know what *Lou* did?" she said in a voice that made it the most important thing of all. Everybody waited to hear.

"No—what?" said Lou, taking out her thumb.

"*She*," said Jane, "caught crabs."

Lou nodded hard. "Yeth," she said. "I caught thum and I killed thum."

"Lou-li," said Madam quickly, "how brave!"

Lou gave her a quick look.

"Ith she my mother, Jane?"

"Yeth," said Madam. "Gracious, children, it's catching."

There was so much laughter no one minded her excuses, and besides they were watching to see what Lou would do. The silly thing only went back to sucking her thumb. All of a sudden Father couldn't stand it, Hood was sent for, and Lou was taken away. Her chair had to go with her because she would not let it go. Then there was silence. And, as Theodore said later, a frightful time was had by all until, after coffee in the chintz sitting room, Madam asked if the trunks had come. Hubert went to see.

"Yeth," he said to try to cheer things up. "They've been dumped on the front stepth."

"Theodore, you and Hubert bring the smallest one in here," said Madam, smiling, "and tell Cook and Gander I want to see them."

No one was expecting presents and no one was looking for them, but when their stepmother began taking out tissue paper after tissue paper from the smallest trunk, it was impossible not to get excited and stare. The first things were for Cook and Gander—rosaries that had seen the Pope and been blessed by him and after that gloves from France. Then the maids could retire. For Theodore and Hubert, hand-knit sweaters from England. Jane's present was two tall bright blue Egyptian cats for book ends; dresses from Holland covered with flowers for Chris and Lou.

They each liked what they got and said so gratefully.

While Jane helped Chris put on her new dress, Madam said: "Now, Edie," and Edie stepped forward and took her box, quite a big one. She took it to the window seat to open, and the others came after her to look. What they saw when she lifted the cover was a mass of bright red. Edie picked up an end. It seemed to be a pair of red trousers.

"For me?" she said, looking at her stepmother.

Madam smiled. "Yes," she said, "if you like them."

Edie turned back the top layer and found a blue jacket and a French cap underneath.

"It's a beret," said Theodore. "Perhaps you'd like to know."

"I know what it is," said Jane suddenly. "I've seen a picture of it in *The National Geographic*. It's a French boy's fishing suit, isn't it?"

"Phweeee!" said Hubert.

Father came over to look, too. "Elsie," he said, "haven't you gone too far?"

In the middle of the blue jacket lay a small package that Edie was pushing with her finger. It was labeled "Cigarettes." Underneath the label it said in much smaller letters "Chocolate." As if that mattered! She took the top of the box and shut it over the costume quickly. Then she put it under her arm and darted through the surrounding circle of bodies, arms, and legs to where her stepmother was sitting. She stood in front of her as stiff as a soldier.

"Anything you want me to do for you for the rest of my life, I'll do," she said, and walked out of the room.

They could hear her going upstairs one at a time on account of her knee, and while they were again admiring their own presents, there were soft thudding noises in the room above. She came down even before the tissue paper was all picked up. The beret was on the side of her head, a handkerchief was at her neck, and there was a cigarette at the side of her mouth.

"Really, Elsie!" said Father.

"You know, children," said Madam, "that these presents are from your father as well as from me."

For once in his life Father was helpless. The boys and

Jane cheered, and to everyone's surprise there was a man's cheer from the hall.

"It's Harry," said Madam, getting up.

"You old rascal," said Father. "Where did you come from and how did you get in?"

"Every door wide open," said Mr. Carpenter, "so I used my feet."

The cheer for Edie went on into a cheer for Mr. Carpenter, and he had to come in, see the presents, say what he had done with Penelope, and promise to stay another week.

"No, no, no," he said. "I only came back to say howdydo and see if I could get a one-man crew for a short cruise Penelope and I are taking to Minimet Bight." He looked Edie up and down in her fisher suit. "It seems like I'll get one with no trouble at all."

Edie ate up her cigarette quickly.

"You mean *me?*" she said.

Mr. Carpenter nodded and continued to inspect her over his glasses. Edie swept off her beret and made him a bow.

"Avec plaisir," she said.

Although it delighted the family and Mr. Carpenter too, Edie herself was not so pleased when she went up to bed soon after, and as she lay on her back trying to stay awake, she began wishing she could do something about that foolish Lou. The reason was that so much good luck all at the same time made her feel queer. Luck always evened up, Theodore said. Suppose she turned out to be a Jonah on Mr. Carpenter's catboat! If she could only fix Lou, *that* would take off the jinx. But Hood had said she was worse than ever. She had come in while Edie and Jane were undressing.

"I can't do a thing with that child," she had said. "Why don't you young ladies try? She keeps saying you're her mother, Miss Edith. I can't stop her."

"Maybe you better *be* her mother," said Jane, "and see what she does then."

"Don't be silly," Edie had said.

But maybe it wasn't a bad idea. She could put on one of Madam's dresses and a big hat, and Madam could put on . . . Oh what? She didn't know. There wasn't anybody in the world the least like her. Edie gave up that idea.

She had another quite soon. Dogs, she thought, know people by the way they smell. Madam smelled of violets. Maybe she could make a "drag" of scent from Lou's room to her mother's and let her follow it like a foxhound. Could foxhound puppies, though, follow a trail or did they have to learn? It wouldn't do any harm to try at least.

Edie found she could not stay awake one minute longer. She wiggled her toes to feel Widgy at the end of her bed, put one hand down to feel the French trousers on the floor beside her and one hand up to touch the cigarettes on the window sill, and was asleep almost before she felt them.

It was one of those nights that only seemed a second until morning, and Edie was sure she had just closed her eyes when she had to open them again because there was a voice almost in her face.

"Mith-thes," it said, "are you awake?"

"Yes, I am," she answered quickly, but amazed that the sun was streaming in. It must be nearly breakfast because

Hood would never let the children out until Father could be heard blowing his nose in the bathroom. She must see if her plan would work as quickly as she could. She slipped out of bed.

"You stay here, Lou," she said, "and take care of Widge. I'll be right back." She plumped Lou into her bed, told Widgy to stay behind, and went to knock at her stepmother's door after she had listened for Father's bath water.

More luck, just more and more luck. No one answered. She was able to go into the empty room and snatch up Madam's bottle of toilet water without any explanation at all. Madam must have gone to see the children just after Lou had come in to see her, and Madam was still there, talking to Hood and Chris probably. Edie was back in her own room like lightning.

"*What* are you doing?" said Jane suddenly, sitting up on her elbows.

"Nothing," said Edie. "Got a handkerchief?"

"No," said Jane, flopping back. "I wish you didn't always have to be so lively in the morning."

Hurry, hurry, thought Edie. Father would be out of the bathroom in a moment. She'd have to use a clean sock.

This she got out of the bureau drawer and soused it with the toilet water. She waved it a little to get the air smelling properly and then dangled it in front of Lou. "Smell," she said.

Lou smelled hard and fell back on the pillows with her hands on top of her nose.

"Go away," she said, "I don't like that big smell."

"What does it smell like?" said Edie. "Can you think? Try it! Come on, try."

"Pigth," said Lou, from under her hands.

"No!" said Edie. "That's not the right thing. I'll hold it further away. Now take a sniff, just a little sniff."

Lou drew in her breath through her hands.

"Mith-thes," she said, "do I smell a skunk?"

"Oh, you old Lou," said Edie, exasperated, "you're no good. Get out of my bed."

"No," said Lou, squirming down further.

"Yes!" said Edie, and she pulled off the bedclothes.

"I hate you," said Lou, getting up and trying to hit her with a fat fist, "and I want my mother, my real mother. You're just an old piece of skunk yourthelf."

"Go and find her then," said Edie. "She's in her room."

"I will do it," said Lou.

As she got to the door, Edie saw Madam coming by. She had on her soft long dressing gown, and her hair was done up in a loose knot at the back of her head. But she wouldn't notice Lou. She swept on by and into her own room. Edie had to follow them both. She didn't see what happened, she was a little too late, but Lou was standing leaning against her mother's knees.

"Do you know who this ith," she said when she saw Edie. She patted her mother's knee. "Ith my own mother, and she smelth *good*."

"Edie, darling," said Madam, "you're a wonder."

The cruise started about eleven o'clock, and Edie went down the path to the shore with Widgy at her heels. He had been granted what Mr. Carpenter called "a special dispensation."

"If Penelope eats him up," he added, "I take no responsibility."

Edie just laughed. Widge wasn't very brave, but he could take care of a cat any old time. Anyway, it was hard not to laugh at everything. She had fixed the luck. There wasn't a cloud in the sky. There was a fair wind. She had on her red trousers and blue jacket. Her cigarettes were in her pocket. And she was missing a week of school. How could everything be better? Maybe she and Mr. Carpenter, after they got going, would decide to sail around the world.